TOO MANY Murphys

To my greatest source of inspiration, my family—Jay, Collette, Jeff, Laura, and Steve.

Library of Congress Cataloging-in-Publication Data

McKenna, Colleen O'Shaughnessy.
Too many Murphys.

Summary: Collette Murphy, eight years old, wishes she were an only child, and is surprised when her wish comes true for a day.
I. Title.
PZ7.M478675To   1988   [Fic]   88-1967

ISBN 0-590-41731-2
11 10 9 8 7 6 5 4 3 2 1   8 9/8 0 1 2 3/9
Printed in the U.S.A.   12
First Scholastic printing, September 1988

TOO MANY
Murphys

Colleen O'Shaughnessy McKenna

SCHOLASTIC
HARDCOVER

Scholastic Inc.
New York

Chapter One

"Just look at this awful hair," cried Collette as she fumbled through her sock drawer. "I am probably the only girl in the third grade, in the whole world, who does not have hair long enough for a ponytail."

Collette pulled a pair of knee socks from the dresser drawer. Brushing back her curly blonde hair, she took two bobby pins and fastened one sock to the left side, the other to the right side.

Collette tossed both socks off her shoulders. That was much better. The socks looked like lovely dark braids.

"I wish my real hair would hurry and grow."

Collette smiled as she added a large yellow barrette to each sock.

1

With a quick spin, Collette turned and faced her tiny class. She nodded to her seven students: Panda Bear and Kitty on the bunk beds, Twinkle Turtle on the stool, and her four best dolls, which leaned against the window atop the radiator.

"We better start making plans for the big science fair," began Collette as she passed out paper and crayons. "Twinkle, are you chewing gum again? Put it in the trash can, please."

Collette pulled out her chair and started to sit. She grinned at the Little Red Riding Hood scene painted on the seat of the chair. Her mother had finished painting it just last night. Mother had said Collette could choose anything in the whole world to be painted on her chair.

Choosing Little Red Riding Hood had been easy. It had been the first book Collette could remember reading all by herself.

"I will need a volunteer to hold the sun," explained Collette. She looked down and checked her list. "And I will need four helpers to hold Saturn, Jupiter, Earth, and Mars."

"Can I hold the sun?" asked Laura.

Collette looked at her younger sister, who was

leaning against the door frame, sucking her thumb.

"Yes, but stop sucking your thumb or you'll smear the poster paint."

"Yippee," cried Laura. She wiped her thumb on her shorts and ran to the dresser to get the sun.

"Can I wear a pair of tall shoes, like you?"

"No. I am the fifty-year-old teacher, so I have to wear them. You hold the sun."

Laura frowned. She set the sun down and crossed her arms and closed her eyes.

Collette groaned. Laura always closed her eyes when she didn't get her own way. It was a four-year-old's way of blocking out the world.

"Let's make a deal, Laura," said Collette. She reached in her dress-up basket and pulled out a long red dress. "You can be the new girl in my class. Let's pretend that you moved here from a big ranch in Texas and you even brought your own horse. You are really, really rich."

Laura's eyes popped open and brightened. "Can I wear this sparkle dress?"

"Sure," said Collette.

3

Laura scrambled out of her shorts and top, her eyes glued to the pearls and beads scattered over the top of the dress.

"Can I ride my horse to school every day?" asked Laura.

"Every day," promised Collette. Grabbing a shoelace from her dresser, she tied the back of the dress together.

"Okay. You can wear my new pink tennis shoes, Laura."

"My horse loves pink!"

"Class, I would like to introduce the new girl," said Collette in a loud, cheerful voice. "Her name is Karen — "

"No, my name is Pinkie."

"Her name is Pinkie, and she just moved here from Texas."

"I'm rich," announced Laura. "I wear sparkle dresses."

Collette seated Laura next to Twinkle and returned to the front of the class.

She took off her sunglasses, shined them on her skirt, and put them back up on the top of her head.

"Teacher," wailed Laura, "can I take off my

dress? My back scratches when I sit down."

Collette closed her eyes and tried to remain calm. She was sure that Laura would not learn one single thing in her classroom.

That made her a little mad. It was much easier to teach stuffed animals and dolls. They always did exactly what she told them to do.

"Keep your dress on, because it's almost lunchtime," replied Collette as she stood to pass out papers.

"Start this math sheet. Color two apples, two oranges, and two raisins while I go figure out your IQ scores," instructed Collette.

Laura hopped off the stool and started scratching her back with her crayon. "Can it be lunchtime now, Teacher? Can I use your kitty-cat furnace?"

Collette gave Laura a blank stare. What was she talking about?

"What furnace?"

"The red furnace in your lunchbox."

Collette started to giggle. "You mean *thermos*. Yes, but don't wreck it."

A loud whack against the door caused it to fly open.

Jeff raced in, rolled across the lower bunk bed, and hid behind it.

"Get out of here!" cried Collette. She grabbed a handful of wrinkled papers from the bed and waved them at Jeff.

Within seconds, Stevie flew into the room. He held a dripping wet pink rabbit in his hand, waving it wildly above his head.

"Where's Jeff?" he shouted. A baseball cap, worn backward on his head, almost covered his eyes.

"He's hiding from you," said Laura, beginning to smile. "Don't look behind the bed, Stevie."

"Give me my rabbit," snapped Collette, snatching it from Stevie's hand. "What did you do to Buttons? He's soaked!"

Stevie hopped from one foot to the other as he tried to get the rabbit back.

"Give me that!"

Collette held it still farther from his reach.

"Get out of my room. Jeff, get out, too."

Jeff's head popped up from behind the bed. He made a face and waved at Stevie before he ducked back below.

"Come here, guy," shouted Stevie, smiling. He

jumped on the bed, knocking Panda Bear on the floor.

"My name is Pinkie," shouted Laura, climbing onto the bed with Stevie. "I have a horse, Stevie. Do you want to see it?"

"Everyone get off my bed!" shouted Collette. "Get out of my classroom."

Jeff rolled out from under the bed, grabbed the wet rabbit from Collette's hand, and shot it across the room.

The wet thunk of the rabbit hit Stevie right on his back.

Stevie turned, laughing as he picked up the rabbit and raced out of the room after Jeff.

Collette slammed her door and leaned against it. Where in the world was her mother? Couldn't she hear how the boys were ruining her day?

"Laura, go downstairs and tell Mommy that the boys are being rude. Tell her to put Stevie in bed for a nap or something. . . ."

Laura stood up, holding her dress with both hands so she wouldn't trip.

"Can I get your furnace, too?"

"Sure, sure," said Collette in a rush. She peered out of her door to see if the coast was clear.

"And don't let the boys see you," whispered Collette.

"Let me wear your tall shoes," said Laura.

"No."

Another forceful whack against the bedroom door jolted Collette. She could hear her brothers laughing in the room down the hall.

Stevie was getting to be just as bad as Jeff. Ever since Stevie had turned two years old, he had been copying everything Jeff said and did.

"Let me wear the tall shoes or I won't go," said Laura, crossing her arms and closing her eyes.

Collette glanced nervously around her room. If she left the room and ran downstairs, the boys would probably sneak in and steal her planets, or toss one of her dolls in the water.

Kicking off her shoes, Collette pushed them toward Laura.

"Oh, all right. Tell Mommy the boys are playing in water and really being bad!"

Laura smiled happily as she slipped into the heels and wobbled down the hall.

"I'll tell her they are being BAD, BAD, and more BAD!" sang out Laura loudly.

Before Collette could shush her, Jeff's bedroom

door opened and both boys raced down the hall to Collette.

"You want to fight?" Jeff asked Collette, dancing backward and forward with his fists raised.

Stevie pushed his hat back and copied Jeff's position, hopping up and down as his fists poked the air.

"You think you're so big, Jeff, just because you're in first grade," said Collette, backing out of the way of Jeff's moves.

Sidestepping her, Jeff darted into her room, grabbing Panda Bear by the ear.

"Come on, Stevie," called Jeff as he ran down the hall.

"Give me Panda," shrieked Collette as she followed the boys into Jeff's room. "Come on, Jeff. Leave my bear alone."

Jeff smiled as he dangled the bear over his large fish tank.

"Don't you dare drop Panda into that disgusting fish tank with all those slimy snails and moss."

Jeff lowered the bear another inch closer to the tank.

"What will you give me?"

Collette eyed Stevie and Jeff. If she made a dash

for the bear, Jeff would be sure and drop him in. Now that he was almost seven he tried to act real cool all the time.

"Are you mad?" asked Stevie. He was beginning to look a little upset.

"Yes," snapped Collette. "And Laura went down to get Mommy, so you both are going to be in so much trouble."

Jeff and Steve exchanged looks.

"Will I have to take a nap?" Stevie's lower lip was beginning to wiggle.

"Yes. A long, long nap, Stevie!"

Just as Stevie was beginning to cry, a heavy thud, followed by a piercing scream, came from the stairwell.

Collette and Jeff bumped into each other as they raced out of his room and down the hall.

The scream had been replaced by a string of "MOMMY-MOMMY-MOMMY!"

Mother was racing up the stairs as Collette raced down. Collette froze as she watched a steady stream of blood trickle from a cut on Laura's forehead.

Laura was rubbing her head with one hand and reaching out for Mother with the other.

"Oh my, oh my!" repeated Collette over and over again.

"You're all right, you're all right," said Mother in a soothing voice as she quickly picked up Laura and studied her for injuries.

Collette tried to swallow, hoping her mother really meant that Laura was all right. Sometimes her mother tried to convince her she was all right when she really was hurt. That way her mother wouldn't go into shock herself.

Jeff tossed Mother a wet washcloth.

"Thanks, honey," said Mother, smiling at Jeff as if he were some sort of a hero.

"Look at this cut! What happened, Collette?" asked Mother. Her voice didn't sound quite as nice now.

"I don't know. I was in Jeff's room . . . where the boys were being really rude . . . and then I heard Laura screaming her head off."

Mother dabbed at the cut with the cloth and frowned.

"Collette is so nice to me," hiccupped Laura, leaning her head against Mother's shoulder. "She let me play school with her. . . . She let me wear her tall shoes. . . ."

Collette stared at one heel lying on the landing. The other shoe dangled from Laura's toes.

Mother glared at Collette as though Collette had given Laura an axe to play with.

"Collette Murphy! Why did you let a little four-year-old go down the stairs with heels on? She could have broken her neck!"

Embarrassment flooded Collette, weighing her down so she couldn't move at all.

"I wanted her to come and get you. The boys were being awful. They ruined my school, stole my animals. . . ."

"There is no excuse for this," said Mother, patting Laura on the back. "I may have to take her for stitches!"

Laura lifted her head and began to cry again.

Collette leaned back to let Stevie run by. He stood next to his mother, suddenly jealous.

"Pick me up, Mommy."

Mother sighed and put her hand on Collette's shoulder.

"Laura looks up to you. All the children do, Collette. I want you to set a good example, all right?"

Collette kept her eyes glued to the floor. She didn't want to talk to anyone.

Mother shifted Laura to her other hip, took Stevie by the hand, and started down the stairs.

"Jeff, if you made a mess in Collette's room, clean it up," said Mother.

Jeff put his hands on his hips and made a face at Collette.

Collette stuck out her tongue and turned her back on him.

She should follow her mother into the kitchen and tell her what awful things the boys were doing to the fish tank. She should tell her that she shouldn't be in the basement painting chairs and stuff when her own kids were falling down stairs and getting into lots and lots of trouble.

Collette tossed both socks away from her face and marched down each step and into the living room.

Just because she was the oldest, she was expected to be some sort of a midget mother.

Pulling out the piano bench, Collette sat down and started to play. She played the same song over and over again. She pressed her foot on the pedal and played as loudly as she could.

No one bothered to come in and tell her to play more softly. No one popped their head around the corner to smile and nod and tell her how well she played for an eight-year-old.

Finally, when even Collette could not bear to hear the song one more time, she stopped.

With a deep sigh, Collette reached out and plunked down the deepest note. She listened to the low, deep tone until it faded.

The vibration shot up her finger and went straight into her heart.

"Too many Murphys," she whispered. "There are too many Murphys in this house."

Chapter Two

There was so much noisy confusion in the house the next morning, Collette almost missed the bus.

First Stevie knocked over his orange juice, which soaked right into Collette's jumper. When she returned in a fresh jumper, she discovered Laura had locked herself in the bathroom, where all of the toothbrushes were kept.

As Collette watched Dad fiddle with a turkey skewer, trying to pop up the bathroom lock, she couldn't help but imagine Marsha across the street.

Marsha was in the third grade, too. They had been friends ever since they were four. She was an only child and usually thought the Murphy house was too crazy to be real. She was always telling Collette that she felt sorry for her, having to live in such a zoo.

Collette sighed. She wouldn't tell Marsha about the bathroom door, or how Stevie dropped his fork into the toaster and blew a fuse.

Right now, Marsha was probably getting ready for school, too. Her mother would be on one side of her, brushing her long dark hair, and her father would be on the other side, handing her a small white towel to dry her hands.

"Bingo!" laughed Daddy as the lock popped. He reached in and pulled out a crying Laura.

"Come here, Shortiecake. Give Daddy a big hug!"

"I was scared, Daddy!" Laura said between sobs. "Jeff told me a big spider was in there with me."

Jeff laughed and raced past, grabbing his toothbrush.

"Watch it," warned Collette, trying to squirm back inside. "I was here first, Jeff."

With three quick brushes, Jeff zoomed out, down the hall, and out the door.

"Bus is here, Collette!" he shouted from the driveway. "Better hurry!"

"Hold the bus!" ordered Mother from the kitchen. "Collette, hurry up. I can't drive you this morning."

Collette felt her stomach tighten up. She hated to run down the street for the bus. Everyone, especially Marsha, would be watching her from the windows, laughing, and glad that they weren't the one running to the bus.

Collette bent her head and charged. The flashing red lights on the bus looked impatient and angry.

"Well, it's about time!" huffed Marsha. She slid over and made room. "Did Stevie hide your book bag again?"

Collette shook her head, too out of breath to speak.

"My mother said she is surprised you don't miss the bus every morning."

Collette tapped her fingers on her book bag and looked out the window. She wasn't about to let Marsha get her mad so early in the morning.

"What are you bringing for the bake sale tomorrow?"

"The what?" asked Collette.

Marsha groaned and nudged Collette with her elbow.

"Don't tell me you forgot! Holy moley, Collette. The third grade bake sale is the only chance we have to raise money for our field trip!"

"Oh, *that* bake sale."

Collette had brought the paper home to show her mother. In fact, she'd tried to give it to her a couple of times. But somebody always fell off a chair, or needed a new roll of toilet paper, or got hungry. Mom would always hold up a finger and say, "Wait a second, honey, I'll be right back."

The paper describing the bake sale was still stuffed in her book bag. Her mother didn't know a thing about it.

"My mother is letting me bring in my special Italian cookies on a real silver tray. The tray is probably worth a couple thousand dollars."

Marsha's voice got louder with each sentence. She looked around the bus to see if anyone was paying attention to her. She always thought everyone loved to listen to her.

18

"The tray has our family monogram on it," continued Marsha in her loud, "look at me" voice.

Collette smiled and nodded to be polite. Her own mom would probably spend the whole day playing with Stevie and Laura. Then she would pop loads of laundry into the washer and try to scrape big wads of gum off the banister.

Even if her mom did know about the bake sale, she wouldn't have time to make cookies.

"My mother and I are making a very rare Italian cookie," explained Marsha.

Then she stopped and gave Collette a fake smile.

"And what in the world are you bringing to the sale?"

Collette sat up straighter and smiled back.

"It's a surprise."

"Ha!" snorted Marsha. "I bet you didn't even tell your mom about the sale. Your mom told my mom she hated to bake."

"A mom doesn't have to like to bake," Collette stated. "Besides, my mom loves to paint."

Marsha giggled.

"Maybe you should bring in a chair to sell."

Collette refused to smile. The two girls sat si-

19

lently as the bus pulled into the school drive.

"Baking is in my mom's blood," continued Marsha in a wistful voice. "I sure am lucky. My mom would never think to buy my birthday cake in a bakery. Or to buy one of those frozen square cakes they keep right next to the peas! Uck! Don't let your mom buy one of those for the sale."

Collette felt a sad tug beneath her jumper. She didn't want Marsha telling the whole third grade that Mrs. Murphy was about to mess up their bake sale.

Suddenly, Collette had a wonderful idea! She sat up straighter and smiled.

"My mother and I are going to bake Irish cookies."

Collette watched Marsha's face, waiting for a reaction. Collette was sure Marsha believed her; she had said it so quickly, it sounded exactly like the truth.

Marsha frowned and shook her head.

"Oh, come on. Every cookie in your house comes straight out of a store bag. I bet your mom doesn't know one recipe by heart."

"She doesn't have to. She's a very good reader. She can read any book in the world. She's going to make a very special batch of cookies tonight."

Marsha crossed her arms and looked smug.

"This I have to see."

Collette lurched forward as the bus came to a quick stop. She grabbed her book bag and stood up in the aisle.

"I'll come over after school and watch," announced Marsha.

"No, it's supposed to be private time with my mom," shot back Collette. She didn't want Marsha poking around their kitchen like a spy.

"I'll give you a dollar if I can come and watch your mom bake," laughed Marsha. She trailed after Collette like a pesty fly.

Collette searched the playground. She had talked to Marsha long enough. Now she needed to find a real friend, like Sarah. Sarah was truly her best friend. She liked Collette a lot, and she didn't even care if Mrs. Murphy liked to bake or not.

There she was! Collette lifted her arm and waved to Sarah. She hugged her book bag to her chest and hurried across the playground.

Things would work out fine. All she had to do would be to go home after school and explain the bake sale to her mother. Once her mother realized the money raised from the sale was going to pay for a terrific field trip, she would be happy to do whatever she could.

Tonight would be so much fun, almost like a party. Daddy could take the little guys out for pizza, and she and her mother would get to work in the kitchen.

Who knew? Maybe after tonight, her mother might decide that she did like to bake, after all.

She could hardly wait to talk to her mother! She would bring in something so special, the whole class would be proud of her!

Chapter Three

"I thought we could make Irish cookies since Grandpa came from Ireland," Collette explained to her mother as soon as she came home from school. "Isn't that a great idea?"

Mother taped a Band-Aid across Stevie's left knee and lifted him down from the counter.

"Uh-huh. . . . Now don't try to ride Jeff's bike, understand, Stevie?"

"Okay."

"All we need is the recipe," continued Collette. She dropped her book bag on the bench and started looking through the cabinets. "Do we have flour, sugar . . . all that baking stuff?"

Mother shrugged. "I don't know. I can always call Daddy to pick up some things on the way home from work. We won't be able to start the cookies until after dinner, anyway."

Collette's shoulders sagged slightly. She had been looking forward to the Irish cookies all day at school. Every time Marsha told another person about her famous Italian cookies on the million-dollar tray, Collette thought about how good her own cookies would be. She was sure that they would sell very quickly. Maybe they would be the first cookies sold.

Her teacher would be proud of her, because Collette Murphy was helping to raise money for the third grade field trip.

"As soon as the other children are watching their after-dinner show, we can come down to the kitchen and get started. In fact, I'll call Daddy right now and see if he can come home early and take the kids to the park. That will give us even more time for the cookies."

Collette gave her mother a tight hug. She may not know too much about baking, but she sure did know a lot about being a good mother.

The whole plan would have worked out perfectly if Daddy had not called to say that he had to work late.

"But Daddy, you have to come home early. You're part of the plan," Collette cried into the phone.

"Sorry, Peanut," said Daddy. "A client flew in tonight and I have to ask him some important questions about my case."

Mother tried to switch their old plans into a new plan. Instead of Daddy taking the kids to the park, Mother gave them a huge tray of chips and dip.

"Wow, a party right in the middle of the week," laughed Jeff. He carried the tray upstairs to the den. "Come on, Laura and Stevie. This will be fun."

Things started out pretty well until Stevie accidentally bit his tongue.

"Pick me up, pick me up," sobbed Stevie as he buried his face into Mother's jeans.

"Hey there, Stevie, you're all right," said Mother as she carefully dabbed at his bloody tongue. "Collette, see if we have a Popsicle in the freezer for Stevie."

Collette hurried to the freezer and pulled out a cherry Popsicle. It was already getting dark outside. If they didn't start the cookies soon, they would never have them ready in time.

"Can we start on the cookies, please, Mom?"

Stevie looked up from his Popsicle and smiled, his teeth already a pale pink. He wiped his tears away with his free hand and squirmed out of Mother's arms.

"I want to help make some cookies!"

Collette frowned. She had been waiting and waiting all day for private time with her mother. She had helped with the dishes, opened the dip and chips, and even found a sack of flour in the pantry.

"I want an apron, too," demanded Stevie. He pointed to Collette's. "I want a red apron like Collette's."

Collette turned and grabbed a fresh bag of pretzels from the pantry.

"Here, Stevie. Take this whole bag of pretzels upstairs and share it with the big guys."

Stevie shook his head, and frowned.

"No, I want to cook some cookies! I'll be a helper."

Collette took a deep breath and drummed her fingers on the tabletop. Things were definitely not working out the way she had planned. She didn't even want to think about Marsha and her mother, across the street, baking their Italian cookies. They wouldn't have a single interruption.

Marsha was probably putting her perfect cookies on her perfect tray, right now.

"Mom," wailed Collette. "Make him go upstairs."

Mother winked at Collette as she swung Stevie onto a high stool.

"Stevie can make Daddy some cookies while we work on our special German cookies."

"Irish cookies," corrected Collette. She watched as her mother handed Stevie a bowl and a spoon. Mother tossed in a handful of flour and added a little bit of water.

"Okay, Stevie," said Mother cheerfully. "You do your work and Collette and I will do our work."

Within seconds, Stevie was clanging his spoon around and around the plastic bowl.

Collette began to feel a little better. Mother was leafing through the cookbook. They had sugar, flour, and eggs. It definitely looked like a real baking group.

"Where are the measuring spoons?" asked Collette as she fumbled through the silverware drawer.

"Oh, I think I gave them to Stevie the other day to use in the sandbox. Use the medicine spoon. It has teaspoons marked on it."

Collette got the large blue plastic spoon from the drawer and handed it to her mother. She couldn't help but smile. Marsha's mother would never have been clever enough to think of using a medicine spoon.

"Did you find a good Irish cookie recipe?" asked Collette cheerfully.

"I found something even better," said Mother brightly.

Collette looked up, worried. That was the same bright voice her mother always used when she was trying to convince her children that the loud thunderstorm outside was really going to be a fun new experience.

Mother bent down and flipped through her cookbook.

"I thought it would be clever to dye oatmeal cookies green. They would look real Irish."

Green oatmeal cookies? What was Irish about that? In fact, if the kids in her class found out that her cookies had nutritious oatmeal in them, they wouldn't buy them at all.

"I don't know, Mom. What's Irish about green cookies?"

"You know how Uncle Joe always wears his plastic green hat on St. Patrick's Day?"

Collette nodded. Uncle Joe was a pretty funny guy. But what did that have to do with her cookies?

"Uncle Joe knows that people call Ireland the Emerald Isle. It makes perfect sense that our cookies would be green."

Collette started to laugh. At last the green cookies were beginning to sound good. Collette felt happier knowing that her cookies rated a special color.

Stevie reached for the food coloring.

"I like this color!"

"No, Stevie," said Mother quickly. She pushed the food coloring away and handed him an egg.

"Yuck!" cried Stevie as he smashed the egg with his fist. "I don't like this egg. It's all broken up."

Mother sighed as she dabbed at the slippery goo.

"Maybe we could make Christmas cookies with green jimmies on them," suggested Collette. "I don't think we have to waste our oatmeal. Besides, I want the kids to buy these cookies!"

Mother tossed the eggshells in the sink and rinsed her hands. Glancing up at the clock, she sighed again.

"Listen, Collette, I am trying to help you with this bake-off, but it's almost bedtime."

Collette giggled.

"It's not a bake-off, Mom, it's a bake sale. . . ."

"Whatever it is, let's get on with it," said Mother, reaching for the cookbook.

Collette felt a sudden sting of tears. She blinked them away. Her mother was trying, she really was.

"I don't want the kids to pass my cookies by, that's all. I want them to look real nice."

"Oh, your friends will buy your cookies, no matter what," said Mother. "Children like cookies, period."

"Friends aren't as loyal today as they were in the olden days," pointed out Collette.

Mother pointed toward Stevie, who was busy trying to bite the cap off the food coloring.

"Get the food coloring away from him, Collette. Now shall I start with the oatmeal cookies? We can either do that or I can call Daddy at the office and ask him to pick up a dozen cookies at the Stop N' Hop."

The thought of getting on the school bus with a box from the Stop N' Hop was awful.

"Everyone in the class is baking homemade cookies," said Collette quickly. "I think it's a rule. Let's go with the oatmeal . . . I mean, Irish cookies. Let's just be sure to make them real green."

"Great idea!" laughed Mother as she cracked the first egg. "Hand me the food coloring and we'll use the whole bottle."

Collette scanned the table. Where was the food coloring, anyway? Mother had just taken it away from Stevie.

Stevie!

Collette groaned so loudly it made her mother jump.

Then they both groaned again as they looked across the table at Stevie.

Green food coloring dripped down from the corners of his mouth. He looked like a vampire frog.

"Yucky!" cried Stevie.

"Oh, Stevie!" wailed Mother as she poured in a cup of oatmeal. "Let me clean you up!"

Collette reached for the spoon and started to stir. Looking up, she could see that it was almost bedtime. Any minute now, Jeff and Laura would pound down the stairs to get a drink of water and tell Mother that the show was over.

Collette pulled the cookbook closer and studied the recipe. She was in the top reading group at school; she was sure that she could follow the recipe.

Collette counted Mother's cup of oatmeal as one and added three more.

The spoon was getting slowed down in the batter, so Collette added a little more water. More water could never hurt a recipe. An oven was so hot that it would evaporate any extra.

When Mother returned with a clean Stevie, Collette was already dropping the batter onto the cookie sheet.

"Well, look at you," said Mother. She smiled at Collette.

"I added the oatmeal and everything," reported Collette proudly. "Three cups."

Mother's smile froze.

"Oh . . . you did? I already added all the oatmeal."

Collette slumped into a chair, frowning at her cookie tray.

"I ruined them!"

Mother set Stevie down and lifted the tray into the oven.

"Of course not. A little extra oatmeal won't hurt. They look wonderful! Let's pop them in and go upstairs to get ready for bed. We can sample them when we come down."

Collette nodded, knowing it was too late to change anything. All she could do now was hope for the best.

Ten minutes later, Collette led the troops down the stairs and into the kitchen.

"It smells good, Collette," said Laura approvingly. "They smell like real cookies."

"They are!" said Mother as she pulled out the cookie sheet.

"I thought they were supposed to be green," said Jeff as Mother set the tray on the counter. "These look gray."

"I painted my face all green," announced Stevie.

"Which used up all our green food coloring," added Mother with a frown.

Collette leaned closer and stared at the cookies.

"They look gray," whispered Collette miserably.

She watched Jeff reach for the largest cookie on the platter. He took a big bite and started to chew and chew . . . and chew.

"Do you like them?" asked Collette in a hopeful voice. "Do they taste okay?"

Jeff shrugged his shoulders, then set the cookie down on the table.

"They're all right. I guess I'm not that hungry."

Laura took a small nibble.

"It tastes good, Collette. Your cookies are like pretty little rocks."

Collette slumped forward, burying her face in her hands.

"They're awful. I know it," she cried. "I can't go to school tomorrow. I just can't show up with a box full of . . . of gray rocks."

"Nonsense," said Mother as she took a bite of Laura's cookie. "These will be fine. They just need a little . . . well, frosting or powdered sugar."

"Maybe a cherry," suggested Laura as she patted Collette on the back.

Mother turned off the oven and took Stevie by the hand.

"Cheer up, Collette. I'll get you kiddos in bed and then I'll whip up a little frosting and bake the rest of the cookies."

"Add a cherry," reminded Laura.

Collette raised her head and managed a smile. A cherry would help.

Jeff tossed his cookie high in the air and caught it. "Sell these as tossing rocks. They're just the right size."

Mother laughed, then stopped and snapped her fingers.

"Hey, that isn't a bad idea, Jeff."

Collette groaned. Now even her mother was making fun of her cookies.

"We can call these cookies Blarney Stones," continued Mother. She was smiling a lot and getting really excited about the whole idea.

"What's a Baloney Stone?" asked Laura.

"Blarney," corrected Mother. "In Ireland, which is where my father was born, they have a huge stone. People believe that if you kiss this stone, you will become a really good talker. You will be able to tell funny stories, remember funny jokes — "

"Like Granddad, right?" asked Stevie.

"Right," agreed Mother. "They call it the 'gift of gab,' which means they will never run out of things to say."

Collette smiled, looking down at the platter of cookies with a little more interest. Her cookies were really sounding important now.

"Up to bed now," said Mother as she lifted Stevie.

Her cookies were going to be all right, after all, thought Collette. Once her mom added the frosting and cherry on the top!

She sure was lucky to have a mom who never went off-duty.

Tomorrow she would be proud to put her Blarney Stones right next to Marsha's Italian cookies.

And they would look great, she just knew it!

Chapter Four

Marsha's mother drove the girls to school the next morning so the Italian cookies on the beautiful silver tray would not get broken.

Collette clutched her shoe box closer to her chest. Inside were her Irish cookies. Even after her mother had tried to fancy them up with frosting and a cherry, they still looked gray. They were so hard that they were in no danger of cracking.

"Let me see your cookies," asked Marsha. She was wearing her very best suede coat to school as though it were her birthday.

"Not now," said Collette. "I want them to be a surprise."

As soon as Mrs. Cessano stopped the car in front of the school, Collette hurried down to the cafeteria. She left her shoe box on the cafeteria table and hurried out before the parent in charge could open it.

As the day passed, Collette kept looking up at the clock on the wall. Soon it would be time for the schoolwork to be put away and the bake sale to begin.

Collette dried her sweating hands on her plaid jumper and crossed her fingers.

"Please, let at least ten or eleven kids buy one of my cookies."

At exactly ten after two, Mrs. Byrnes told the class to put away their math booklets and get out their money for the bake sale.

"At last," Roger called out. "I'm starving."

The class gave a cheer and lined up by the door.

As Collette got out her change purse, she tried to swallow. It was no use. She was so nervous about everyone seeing her cookies that she had simply run out of anything wet in her mouth.

"Wake up, Collette," sang out Marsha as she jingled her small change purse in Collette's face. "My mother gave me four dollars! She said that I could get something special for dessert tonight."

"That's nice, Marsha. I have two dollars."

"I think I'll just buy back some of my Italian cookies," whispered Marsha. "I just hope that there are some left when I get down there. I bet all of the seventh- and eighth-graders bought them."

Collette smiled weakly. She was sure that her cookies would still be there, stacked in a high gray tower to the sky.

The third-graders paraded down the hall to the cafeteria, shaking their change purses like sleigh bells.

Inside the cafeteria, volunteer moms stood behind tables, smiling and eager to help with the bake sale.

"I wonder where the Italian section is?" asked Marsha as she studied the cookie-filled tables.

Collette shook her head and started to walk up and down the aisles. She stopped in front of a cake baked in the shape of a lamb, its fleece made from fluffy white coconut. Two black jelly-bean eyes stared up at Collette.

"You're too cute to eat," laughed Collette. She couldn't buy the lamb cake. She knew Stevie and Laura would try to sleep with it instead of eating it.

Sarah came up and stood beside Collette. She groaned and started to laugh.

"I am soooo embarrassed, Collette. The cake my dad made last night is really sick. The top layer is sliding off the top."

Collette looked over at the cake and laughed.

"I'll buy it, Sarah. My brothers and sister won't know the difference. I bet it tastes great."

Collette bought the cake and smiled, feeling very loyal. Sarah had been her best friend for almost a year. They never fought over a single thing. Their friendship was too special for that.

She still didn't see her cookies anywhere. Maybe they looked so awful the mothers in charge didn't even put them out.

"Oh, look at the Italian cookies," squealed Marsha in a voice loud enough for a school play.

Collette walked closer and examined the cookies on the silver tray. They really did look wonderful.

"Hey, Marsha, your cookies smell funny — like a doctor's office," jeered Roger. "Are you sure there isn't some chemical in there we should all know about . . . like bug spray?"

Several children started to laugh. Collette and Sarah didn't join in when they saw Marsha shove her hands on her hips and blow her bangs straight up in the air.

"It's called anise, and it's a very special and expensive spice, you dope!" hissed Marsha. "What did you bring in for the sale, Roger? I bet you brought in those gray lumpy cookies over there, because they look just like your head!"

Roger's mouth fell open, and children started to laugh again.

Collette did not even smile. Her heart was beating so fast that she looked down at her jumper to make sure it wasn't moving up and down.

The whole class was laughing at her cookies!

Stop laughing at my mom's cookies! she wanted to scream. My mom tried her absolute best. She's a painter, not a baker.

Mrs. Byrnes picked up the lid that lay beside the cookies. She held it up to show the class.

On the inside was a beautiful picture of leprechauns and shamrocks. In green marker, Mrs.

Murphy had neatly printed: BLARNEY STONES!

"Mrs. Murphy drew that," announced Marsha. "I know her artwork."

Collette blushed as everyone began talking about how great the picture was.

"Can you eat Blarney Stones?" asked Peggy.

Mrs. Byrnes jumped right into being a teacher and told the whole class about the legend of the Blarney Stone.

"Maybe you should all buy a cookie so you'll do a good job talking about your book reports this afternoon."

The children laughed as though Mrs. Byrnes were joking. But half of them lined up and bought one anyway.

In less than five minutes, the shoe box was empty. The kids were probably used to teachers telling the truth all the time and didn't want to take any chances.

Collette got a drink from the water fountain. She turned and looked up and down the aisles. Now that her cookies were gone she could relax and enjoy herself.

Marsha had her arms crossed, standing next to her silver tray.

"Roger has scared everybody away from buying my cookies."

Unsnapping her change purse, Collette pulled out sixty cents.

"I was just coming over to buy six for dessert at our house."

Marsha glared at the cake box Collette was holding, but scooped seven cookies off the tray and handed them to Collette.

"Here, you can have one free . . . since they're so good."

"Time to go," called Mrs. Byrnes from the door. "Line up."

As the third-graders filed past the office, they slowed to watch a sixth-grader tacking up a poster.

ATTENTION PARENTS!
DON'T FORGET
OPEN HOUSE
TUESDAY 9:00 A.M.–11:00 A.M.
ALL ARE WELCOME TO ATTEND

Collette gave a little laugh. She could hardly wait for Open House. Mrs. Byrnes had picked a lot of her artwork to hang in the hall. And her English essay was hanging right on her locker with a big star on the top.

Her dad was trying hard to finish up a trial so he would be able to come this year. Usually he missed a lot of daytime stuff because judges didn't give you free days, not even if you brought in a note from home.

This year her mother was going to ask Mrs. Withers to baby-sit the little guys so she could concentrate on all of Collette's papers. She said she wanted to look at everything because she was very proud of Collette's hard work.

Collette opened her locker and put her baked goods inside. It would smell so sweet and good when she got them after school.

"Open House . . . yuck!" whined Marsha as she slammed her locker door. "I guess we'll have to clean our desks!"

"Come on," laughed Collette as she pulled her toward the door.

Cleaning a desk was worth it. She was so excited she would have cleaned the whole school.

Open House was going to be as special as a party!

44

Chapter Five

The following Tuesday, Collette was impatient, anxious for Open House to begin. She tried to swallow a yawn. Marsha had been talking nonstop since she got in the classroom.

"You won't believe where my mother is taking me after school to celebrate Open House," continued Marsha.

"Where?"

Marsha's mother celebrated just about everything in the whole world if it involved Marsha. Being an only child must really be an easy job.

"You won't guess in a hundred years," added Marsha.

Collette kept washing the top of her desk. She wanted it spick-and-span for Open House.

Besides, Marsha never waited for anyone to answer her questions. She just took it for granted that they were still listening.

"This is really going to crack you up, Collette!" Marsha pounded her desk top with her fist as she began to laugh all over again. "My crazy mom is taking me to buy a pair of purple jeans, a purple sweater, and even some purple socks. Mom thinks I am going to look like a walking plum! You know my mom, she celebrates everything!"

"Marsha, aren't you going to clean out your desk for Open House? It's almost nine o'clock!"

Marsha's desk was an absolute mess. Pencils and paper scraps were sticking out of it all the way around.

Collette opened her own desk, rechecking the neat stacks of books and papers. She touched the pencils, bound with a fat, red rubber band.

Having your own desk was one of the nicest things about school. You didn't have to share it with anyone. Collette loved the fact that once she put something in her desk, it would stay exactly that way until she reached in the next day to change it.

Collette pictured her own little white desk at

home. If she opened any drawer she would probably find some of her brother's rubber spiders and snakes or Laura's tiny dolls peeking out.

"Would you like me to help you clean out your desk real fast?" offered Collette. She hated the thought of a perfectly fine desk being in such a mess.

Marsha shook her head as she flung open her desk top.

"It doesn't look too bad to me. I think I just need to trim it up a bit."

Marsha bent over her desk, raking everything into the center. Putting her largest books on top, she created a flat effect.

"This will be fine," said Marsha with a grin.

Collette watched in disbelief as Marsha grabbed handfuls of used pencils and crayons and tossed them in the waste can.

Collette eyed the crayons. Stevie and Laura sure would love using them when they played school.

"Is your mother bringing the whole crew this morning?" asked Marsha.

Collette smiled, very pleased.

"No. My mother promised that she would get a sitter. I heard her talking to Mrs. Withers last night. She said that she would love to baby-sit for us."

"You should let Stevie come," laughed Marsha. "He is really a funny kid."

"I don't like people laughing at him on school property."

Sarah walked over to the girls and sat down in Marsha's seat.

"Well, my desk looks great. I'm all ready. My grandmother may come with my mom. I just hope she doesn't embarrass me by bringing a camera!"

"My mother is getting a baby-sitter so she can concentrate on my schoolwork," confided Collette. "My mother is excited about coming today. My dad couldn't come because his client's trial is still going on. He wants to hurry up and finish it before his birthday dinner."

The large white clock ticked silently on the wall above the teacher's desk. Open House was going to start in fifteen minutes.

Collette sat back in her desk, wiping her hands across its clean surface. There was nothing to do now but sit and wait.

Parents started arriving at exactly nine o'clock.

Some leaned against the chalkboard, while others tried not to look too uncomfortable on the small chairs arranged in a semicircle.

A bright flash went off as Sarah's grandmother snapped a picture.

The classroom was getting crowded. Mothers and fathers were peering around the room, smiling when they spotted papers belonging to their child.

Collette checked the clock again. Nine-thirty. Her mother was probably just a little late because she had to pick up the baby-sitter. She was probably kissing Laura and Stevie good-bye this very minute, jingling her car keys and anxious to get to Collette's Open House.

Collette smiled. Her mom would be one of the prettiest moms if she fixed her hair fancy and used some of the makeup in her cosmetic bag.

It would be nice to have her mother all to herself for a few hours. She knew she had to share her with Jeff, in the first grade. But while her mother was in her homeroom, she wouldn't have to share her with anyone!

Mrs. Byrnes blew on the pitch pipe, signaling the beginning of the first song.

Everyone sat up straighter.

Mrs. Byrnes raised both arms high in the air and nodded.

The class lifted their heads and began the opening song for the parents.

"I am a . . . happy wanderer," they sang.

"That's my whistle!" shouted a voice from the back of the room.

Heads turned to see who had interrupted the song. Collette stared straight ahead, her hands locked tightly together. She didn't have to turn around to know that the voice belonged to Stevie!

Why weren't the little guys home with a baby-sitter like they were supposed to be?

Mrs. Byrnes started singing more loudly, drawing those children who had stopped singing to stare at Stevie back into the song.

When the song was over and guests were clapping, Collette twisted in her seat to frown at the little Murphys in the back of the classroom.

"Hi, Collette!" said Laura loudly.

"Where's Collette?" demanded Stevie. "I can't see her."

Mrs. Murphy dove into her purse and brought out two pretzel sticks.

"Your little brother looks like an angel with his blond curls," whispered Sarah, from behind Collette.

Collette shook her head, watching Stevie out of the corner of her eye. She couldn't agree with Sarah about the angel part. Actually, he was more like a time bomb.

Sooner or later you knew he would go off.

The class was in the middle of the second verse of their school song when Collette saw Stevie slide off Mother's lap. Mother reached into her purse and handed him a coloring book and a pack of crayons.

Good! At least her mother remembered to bring something to keep him out of trouble.

Then Mother turned to help Laura find her place on the song sheet they were sharing.

Laura looked extra pretty with her ribbons and party dress.

Actually things weren't going so badly, thought Collette. She reached inside her desk for the tambourine she would be using during the next song.

The baby-sitter probably canceled at the last minute, and there wasn't anything to do but buff up the little guys and bring them along.

The third song was filled with bells, banjos, and tambourines. Collette grinned, knowing that Stevie and Laura would love this song the best.

She glanced behind her, hoping they were enjoying themselves.

Stevie was no longer there. Mother and Laura were clapping their hands in time to the music with the other guests.

To the left of the guests tiptoed Stevie. He moved quietly toward the front of the room, his eyes glued to the large round globe that sat in its stand next to the teacher's desk.

Collette picked up her tambourine and shook it loudly, even though it wasn't time.

Surely Mother would look her way so she could warn her that Stevie was heading for the globe.

Collette shook the tambourine again. She shook it so violently that her elbow banged against her desk top.

Mrs. Byrnes gave Collette a slight frown and shook her head. Collette was not supposed to shake the tambourine for another five measures.

Mother sang and clapped, never looking up.

Stevie reached the globe, putting both hands on its surface to feel its smoothness.

Mrs. Byrnes looked over and smiled at Stevie. She gave him a happy nod, glad that he no longer wanted her pitch pipe.

Mrs. Byrnes turned and moved more closely to the bell section, encouraging them to ring loudly.

Stevie reached out both hands and quickly put the globe on the floor. The globe rolled a few inches and stopped. Stevie giggled.

Collette bit her lip and groaned. She could tell by the gleam in Stevie's eyes that he considered the globe a great new toy.

She turned to face Mother and gave one last mighty shake of her tambourine. It was no use. Mother was now fixing Laura's left bow.

"Stevie!" hissed Collette.

Stevie looked up. When he saw Collette, he smiled. "Hey, Collette. Watch my trick!"

"No!" cried Collette, dropping her tambourine to the floor.

With one mighty kick, Stevie propelled the globe down the aisle.

Laughing aloud at his success, he chased the globe, kicking it soccer-style around the room.

"Stevie Murphy!" cried Mother from the back.

Singing had stopped. Mrs. Byrnes looked up

and gasped, nearly swallowing her pitch pipe.

Collette stared down at her desk, wishing it were big enough for her to crawl inside.

Mother reached Stevie and the globe seconds before Mrs. Byrnes.

"I'm so sorry," began Mrs. Murphy. "Just look at this awful dent near the South Pole."

Mrs. Byrnes took the globe and frowned.

"It won't show too much when it is back where it belongs."

As Mrs. Byrnes walked past Stevie, she chose the wrong time to scold him.

"No, no, little boy. You must not play with the school's globe."

"No fair. I got the ball first!"

The class laughed.

Roger leaned over and poked Collette with his pencil.

"Your little brother is louder than a fire alarm!"

If only a real fire alarm would go off, Collette thought. She kept her eyes down, but she could hear Stevie begging for one more kick and her mother trying to get him to the back of the room.

The kids were trying not to laugh too loudly because they knew their parents were in the room.

The parents were trying just as hard because of their kids.

Collette did not feel like laughing at all. It was her brother who was ruining Open House.

Things calmed down as Mrs. Byrnes began to explain the science experiment.

"In science today we will be doing a bit of magic. We will change these dirty pennies into shiny pennies. All we need are ordinary household products: salt, vinegar, and plain tap water."

In a dramatic flourish, Mrs. Byrnes lifted the jar of dirty pennies high into the air.

"Can I have some dirty pennies?" wailed a voice from the back.

Collette's spine began to stiffen. She stared at Mrs. Byrnes, trying to look as involved as possible.

Sarah covered her mouth and giggled. That bothered Collette a little. She didn't think good friends should laugh at each other's families.

Collette jerked her body to the right and watched as her mother emptied out her change purse. She handed Stevie nickels and dimes as fast as she could.

Stevie glared at his handful of money. Then he looked at the big jar of dirty pennies.

"I want dirty monies!"

Stevie pointed to Mrs. Byrnes.

Mrs. Byrnes turned slightly away and started to talk more loudly.

"Let's divide into groups of four — "

"I want two dirty pennies!" cried Stevie.

Collette's hands were beginning to sweat. That was a sure sign that she was about to die of embarrassment.

From behind her, Collette could hear a small chair being knocked over.

"I don't want to go," wailed Laura. "I was good."

Mrs. Murphy stood and took each little Murphy by the hand, steering them out of the classroom.

Collette stared at her clean desk top. Her mother never even got a chance to see how nice and neat it was.

The classroom suddenly seemed too quiet.

Mrs. Byrnes went on with the science experiment. Collette only went through the motions. She couldn't stop thinking about her family messing up the Open House.

She had planned that this Open House was going to be the most fun of all. A perfect time for Collette and her mother to share a morning.

It was all Stevie's fault. He was always getting in trouble, and usually Collette couldn't stay mad at him.

It was hard to stay mad at someone so young. He didn't even know all his colors.

But this time Stevie had gone too far. He had ruined the whole Open House by being loud and rude.

Mrs. Byrnes was mad, too. Collette knew it. She didn't even ask Collette to pass out the new tablets or to empty the pencil sharpener.

Mrs. Byrnes was probably sure she had been around too many Murphys for one day.

Collette straightened out her desk at the end of the day, even though it was still neat as a pin.

She kept the top opened for a long time, hoping Mrs. Byrnes would walk by and say, "Why, Collette, this is the neatest desk I have seen in a long time."

But she didn't.

As the buses were being called, Collette walked slowly past Mrs. Byrnes's desk.

Maybe she should stop and offer some sort of an apology. She could remind her teacher that Stevie was only two years old.

"Good-night, Mrs. Byrnes," she began. "I just wanted to. . . ."

Mrs. Byrnes looked up from her lesson plan book and smiled.

"Oh, Collette . . . just the person I wanted to see."

Collette was sure her heart was about to stop. What if Mrs. Byrnes was going to give her a detention for having a family that ruined Open House?

Mrs. Byrnes reached into her center drawer and pulled out a plastic bag filled with dirty pennies.

"These were the leftovers. I thought you could take them home to your brother."

"Thank you," said Collette slowly. "He'll love them."

She waited to see if Mrs. Byrnes wanted to mention how Stevie also ruined her Open House. But she didn't.

Collette turned and hurried across the classroom.

Mrs. Byrnes was probably giving her the pennies to take to Stevie so he wouldn't try to come back for them.

Collette shifted her book bag and gripped the

plastic bag filled with pennies tightly as she walked down the hall to the bus.

She'd give Stevie the pennies, but only after she told him how naughty he had been. He was never allowed to come to another Open House in his whole life.

She felt like being mad at everyone in the whole house, but she knew she couldn't. Tonight was her dad's birthday, and a bad mood was probably the worst present you could give someone.

She tried to smile as she climbed onto the bus, thinking of the wonderful present she had made for her dad.

He would love it. She had made it for him all by herself. It would probably be his best present.

As the bus pulled away, Collette decided to give him another present. She wouldn't even mention how awful Open House had been, or act a bit sad that the judge wouldn't let him come to see it.

Even though her Open House day had been just plain awful, nothing would go wrong with his birthday.

She'd watch Stevie and the others like a hawk, making sure they were good.

Birthdays were too special to ruin!

Chapter Six

On the bus ride home, Collette could not stop thinking about how Stevie had messed up Open House.

She wouldn't bother her dad about it, because of his birthday. But she could hardly wait to ask her mother why she had brought the little guys to school.

"You could have asked Gramma to baby-sit," said Collette. "When Mrs. Withers said she had the flu and couldn't come, then you should have called — "

"I did, I did . . ." said Mother quickly. She dug deeper into the frosting can. "Who ate part of this frosting? I'm not going to have enough for Daddy's cake. Gramma was playing bridge with her group. Oh, phooey, I'm out of frosting!"

"Jeff ate it," laughed Stevie.

"No way," said Jeff. "You did, Stevie. I see chocolate on your chin."

Collette handed Mother the candles.

"I bet Mrs. Foster would have baby-sat if you had asked her. She's always saying that Stevie and Laura are so cute."

"Actions speak louder than words," said Mother with a small grin.

Collette frowned. She didn't like it when her mother talked like a Chinese fortune cookie.

"Can I light the candles?" asked Jeff. "I'll be careful."

Jeff took the matches.

"Not yet. Daddy isn't even home."

Mother took the matches away from him and put them in her pocket.

"You didn't even get a chance to see how clean my desk was," continued Collette, her voice dropping down to a whisper. "And I made a fancy name card and taped it to the — "

"Mom, Stevie put his tongue on the cake!"

shouted Laura. "I see the wet spot!"

"Stevie!" snapped Mother, lifting him down from the counter. "Go play. Stay away from the cake."

"Did you hear me play the tambourine?" asked Collette. She edged closer to her mother. "That was the first time I ever played it."

"You were wonderful," said Mother. She bent down and kissed Collette. "Maybe you can sing that nice song after dinner."

"When is Daddy coming home?" asked Laura.

"Yeah, I wrapped Daddy up some dirty pennies," added Stevie. "For his birthday present."

Collette glared at Stevie, remembering the Open House all over again.

"Is Daddy inviting any of his friends to the birthday dinner?" asked Laura.

"We're his friends," said Jeff.

"We are having one special guest," said Mother. She smiled and winked at Collette. "I called Sarah and invited her. She'll be here any minute."

"Sarah!" Collette laughed and hugged her mom. What a great surprise. Her mother must have known how sad she had been about Open House.

"Let's go finish wrapping the presents," suggested Collette, suddenly excited about the party ahead.

"I'm glad Sarah is coming for dinner," said Laura as she followed Collette out of the room and up the stairs. "Mommy always has fancy food when company comes."

"Stevie will show off for Sarah," said Jeff. "You better watch out for him, Collette."

"I will." Collette led the others into her room. She picked up a small box and added a bright green bow. "I hope Daddy likes my present."

"He will," said Laura. "But what if Daddy already has an orange juice can?"

Collette frowned. "I told you, it's not an orange juice can, Laura. It's a fancy pencil can for his desk at work."

"Do you want a few of my crayons to put in the can?"

"Daddy doesn't use crayons at work," said Jeff. "He doesn't go to kindergarten, you know."

"Well . . . I know. But if Daddy does all of his work, I bet he is allowed to color then, right?" Laura's voice was a little shaky and her eyes were getting wet-looking.

"Oh sure, sure." Collette almost forgot how important these things were to a four-year-old. Not being able to color must seem like the worst punishment in the world.

"Add a ribbon to your package and let's go downstairs and put these presents with the others," said Collette.

The three children walked downstairs carrying their presents.

RRRRRRRRRRRRRipppppppp!

"What's that?" asked Jeff, looking around the room.

"Maybe it's a robber, ripping up money," whispered Laura.

Collette set her present down and walked slowly to the yellow couch. Leaning over the back, she saw Stevie. He sat on the floor, carefully removing every shred of paper from all of Daddy's birthday presents.

"Stevie Murphy!" cried Collette. "What do you think you're doing?"

Stevie dropped the present he was holding and stood up.

"You're not allowed to open Daddy's presents!"

shouted Jeff, putting his face close to Stevie's. "You're in trouble, kid."

Laura snatched her present from the pile and held it close to her.

"You're not going to open this one, Stevie!"

Stevie climbed over the back of the couch. He tightened his fists into balls of determination.

"Give me that present, Laura," demanded Stevie as he stomped toward her.

Laura's eyes flew open. She turned and quickly ran out of the room. Stevie gave a yelp and chased after her.

Collette and Jeff began picking up the scraps of paper.

"I hope Stevie doesn't make trouble when Sarah comes," said Collette.

Laura raced back into the room, her sweatshirt bulging.

"I hided my present from Stevie."

The three of them started to laugh.

Collette went into the dining room and studied the table. It looked beautiful. Mother had even used the fancy napkins and napkin rings.

"I don't believe your father is so late on his

special night. I wanted him to be here before Sarah arrived," said Mother as she hurried into the dining room. "I have a fish in the oven that is getting drier by the minute."

"Stevie unwrapped most of the presents, Mom," reported Collette. "I hid the rest in the closet."

"Maybe we should take the presents out and put Stevie in the closet," said Mother with a grin.

Collette grinned back, glad that mothers were so easy to cheer up.

The doorbell chimed its three stair-step tones.

"Sarah's here!" cried Collette.

Sarah walked in, handing Mrs. Murphy a box of candy.

"Hello, Mrs. Murphy. Sorry I'm a little late. This is for Mr. Murphy's birthday!"

The phone rang while Collette was showing Sarah how nice the table looked. Real flowers in a crystal vase sat in the middle. It looked fancier than any restaurant.

"Your father just called. He had engine trouble, but he is on the way home now."

Fifteen minutes later, Daddy walked through the door. He acted extra cheerful because he knew he was so late.

"We better eat right away," suggested Mother. She hurried back to the kitchen.

"Daddy!" wailed Laura from the doorway. "I have been hiding your present all night. Don't you want to open it?"

"Oh sure," said Daddy, reaching down and taking a present from the coffee table. He opened it quickly.

"Oh, Laura, new socks . . . just what Daddy needed!"

Laura leaned against the wall and messed up her hair.

"No fair. You didn't open mine. That was Jeff's present!"

Jeff laughed. "Dad likes me best, right, Dad?"

Collette reached over and pulled Laura's present from under her sweatshirt. She wanted to get Laura back in a good mood before Sarah thought her family was a bunch of crybabies.

She looked over at Sarah to see if she was bored already. But Sarah was showing Stevie pictures from a magazine.

Daddy pulled Laura onto his lap as he unwrapped her present.

Collette helped Daddy with the tape and paper.

She wanted to hurry up things so Sarah wouldn't get too hungry.

Daddy lifted a painted Popsicle stick from the paper. He said it was the nicest stick he had ever seen. Then Mother called everyone into the dining room.

"Sit next to me, Sarah," suggested Collette.

"Me, too," cried Stevie. He reached out and grabbed her hand.

"I love your house," said Sarah as she looked around the large dining room. "It must be a hundred years old. Maybe we could play *Little Women* in here sometime."

"Sure," said Collette. She reexamined the room herself. It was big all right, but certainly not as modern as Sarah's apartment.

Jeff helped Mother carry in casserole dishes.

"Peas, hot peaches with cinnamon," said Daddy as he looked inside each dish. "What a great dinner."

Mother winked at Collette and Sarah. Daddy was trying extra hard to love everything.

Mother lit the candles on the table.

Stevie opened his mouth and started to sing:

"Happy Birthday time to me. . . ."

Sarah started to laugh. Collette laughed, too. Stevie seemed pretty funny when he wasn't ruining things.

Mother walked slowly in from the kitchen, carrying a large silver platter. She set it in front of Daddy.

"Flounder," said Daddy, pleased. "You cooked a whole fish!"

Collette was glad her dad liked his special dinner. Her mother must have read two or three cookbooks to learn how to cook a whole fish.

The large fish lay quietly on the platter, surrounded by a hedge of green parsley.

Everyone leaned closer to get a good look at the fish.

Suddenly Stevie hid his face in his napkin.

"Is that a real eyeball?" asked Jeff. "It's staring at me like it knows me."

"No, it is not real," laughed Mother. "I used a grape for the eye."

"Is the real eye smashed under the grape?" asked Laura.

Sarah shuddered beside Collette.

Collette began to worry all over again. What if Sarah was beginning to lose her appetite? What if she wanted to just go home?

Daddy lifted the knife and began to cut the fish.

"Yikes!" shouted Stevie from behind his napkin. "Don't kill the snake!"

"It's a fish, Stevie," corrected Jeff. "And it's already dead. Mommy killed it in the kitchen."

Stevie pointed to the platter.

"Fix the poor fish, Daddy."

"It is too dead, Stevie," explained Laura. "Right Mommy?"

Mother stood up at the end of the table. She walked over to Daddy and took the knife from his hands.

"Everything is getting cold."

She quickly cut off the fish's head and pushed it to the side of the platter. She cut the fish into eight neat squares and laid the knife down.

"Yuck," whispered Laura, her eyes glued to the head of the fish.

Stevie slid off his chair and hid under the table.

Mother said a blessing and placed a serving of fish, peas, and hot peaches on each plate.

The plates were passed around the table in silence.

"Looks good, looks great," said Daddy after a long pause.

Collette looked around the table. All of the kids, including Sarah, were staring at the platter.

The fish head, half hidden in the forest of parsley, seemed to be staring up at the ceiling in defeat.

"Let's start enjoying this nice dinner that your mother has prepared," said Daddy in a stern voice.

He looked around the table, noticing that no one had picked up their fork.

"I mean it," he added, giving the fish platter an impatient shove.

This was enough to send the fish head deeper into the parsley. The grape jiggled and flew off the platter. It rolled across the table, past the flowers, and stopped right next to Sarah's water glass.

Sarah smiled weakly at the grape, which really did seem to be staring right back at her.

"Goodness, what next?" said Mother in a low voice. She put down her fork and looked very tired.

Collette looked over at her mother. She knew

just how she felt. Sometimes, no matter how hard you plan for something to work out perfectly . . . it just doesn't.

Reaching across Sarah's plate, Collette quickly picked up the grape.

She didn't think about how much the grape felt like a real eyeball; she just smiled bravely at her mother as she quickly popped it into her mouth and swallowed it.

Collette reached for her water glass and smiled.

"It's a grape, all right!" she said.

Sarah and Mother laughed. Soon everyone started to laugh. Sarah picked up her fork and took a big bite of fish.

"It's delicious, Mrs. Murphy!"

Stevie crawled out from under the table. He watched Sarah chew for several minutes before he stabbed his fish with his fork.

"This is good," declared Stevie. He picked up a handful of peas and popped them into his mouth like peanuts.

Daddy finished his fish and asked who wanted to play Twenty Questions.

"What is that?" asked Sarah.

"My dad goes around the table and asks twenty

questions. It's fun," explained Jeff.

Sarah took another bite of fish and smiled.

"You're lucky you have such a big family, Collette. Twenty Questions at my house would be boring. It must be fun to live here."

Collette studied Sarah's face, wondering if she was making some sort of a joke.

She had to be.

After all, nothing could be more perfect than being an only child.

Collette closed her eyes as Mother brought out Daddy's birthday cake. Now was the perfect time to make her own wish.

"I wish I could be an only child," she whispered. "Just to see how special it really feels."

She opened her eyes and smiled through the rising gray smoke above the candles.

Good! Daddy had blown out all of the candles with one breath. That was a sure sign that all their wishes would come true.

Chapter Seven

The next day at school, Collette opened her lunchbox, glad to find a big piece of birthday cake from the night before.

"Did your mom bake that?" asked Marsha as she peered at Collette's lunch.

"Yes. It's part of my dad's birthday cake."

"It even has a rose on it," muttered Marsha as she took a bite of her sandwich. "Your mom sure does like to bake all of a sudden. My mother read an article in a magazine the other day. It told all about how too much sugar can rot your teeth and blood."

"You're crazy," laughed Sarah. "Collette's mom only bakes for birthdays and bake sales, right Collette?"

74

Collette divided the cake into three sections. "Here, have some."

Sarah took the end piece with the small yellow rose. "I got a rose last night, too."

Marsha put her sandwich down with a thwack.

"Last night? What do you mean, last night? Did you guys have some sort of a party without me?"

"Sarah came over for my dad's birthday dinner."

Marsha sat up straighter and frowned.

"Well, thank you very much for including me!"

"I've had you over for dinner at least three hundred times, Marsha."

Marsha crumpled up her sandwich in its plastic bag.

"You have never, ever invited me for a birthday dinner! In fact, most of the times, we just have leftovers when I come over."

Sarah and Collette exchanged puzzled looks. It was impossible to please Marsha.

"Oh, never mind," sighed Marsha. "Anyway, I have more important things to think about. Just think, after lunch, Mrs. Byrnes will be picking the roles for the Christmas play."

"I just hope Mrs. Byrnes didn't write a love scene or anything," giggled Sarah. "I would just

75

die if I had to call someone as disgusting as Roger 'Honey' or 'Sweetheart.' "

The girls leaned closer, giggling at the thought of it.

"Hey, Marsha," yelled Roger from the end of the table. "If you get a big part in the play, we'll have to rate it X . . . 'cause you're extra awful!"

Roger's friends began to hoot and laugh.

"Too bad your mother had to go and find you at a rummage sale," Marsha jeered. Then she swung around and turned her back on Roger.

"I have my own private tape recorder," said Marsha. "So when I get the lead, I can record all of my lines into it. Then I can listen to it as I fall asleep. My second mind will retain it all."

Collette chewed thoughtfully on her sandwich. Marsha had just about everything you could want in a bedroom.

She had her own TV, stereo, and even her own bathroom. It was complete with tiny towels monogrammed with a big "M."

"You can come over whenever you want, Sarah," offered Marsha. "I have a double canopy bed if you want to spend the night."

It was getting harder for Collette to listen to this conversation any longer. Marsha had so many terrific gadgets in her house. And she sure didn't have any brothers and sisters running around.

"Oh, I just have to get the lead in that play. I have a lot of theater in my blood," explained Marsha, waving a celery stick lazily in the air. "My aunt used to get all the leads in the college plays."

"That's great," said Collette.

Marsha took a bite of celery and shook her head. "It was, until some jealous person complained to the director. They were jealous because my aunt was so talented. The director got nervous because this jealous person had gobs of friends. He was afraid the whole drama department would go on strike. Then he would have to paint the scenery and smear makeup on the actors and sew costumes . . . all by himself."

"What happened?"

"The director fired my aunt."

Marsha scowled at the memory of it all.

"So instead of my aunt acting in Walt Disney movies, she dropped out of college and married my Uncle Ed."

Marsha took another bite of celery.

"So now, thanks to that awful director, my aunt is a dental assistant!"

Sarah and Collette looked at each other and began to giggle.

"I certainly don't see anything funny in this story, which is perfectly true."

"I know it isn't funny," laughed Collette, beginning to laugh harder than ever. "But, instead of starring on television, your aunt is busy scraping plaque off some little kid's teeth."

Sarah started to hiccup with laughter. She tried to giggle her way to a stop.

Marsha snapped her lunchbox shut.

"This is the last time I trust you two with a family secret. Let's go outside."

The three girls stood and walked out onto the playground. It was fun talking about the play.

Collette was glad that Sarah was interested in doing scenery, too. It would be a lot of fun to work on it together.

After lunch, the class became very quiet as Mrs. Byrnes passed out the scripts.

"There is a part for everyone. Some parts seem larger than others, but that isn't really true. If you have fewer lines, then you will be doing more art-work."

"Will we have time to get in character before the auditions?" asked Marsha. "I'm at my best then."

"I didn't know you had a best," shouted Roger.

"The main character in the play is a girl named Hannah Johnson," explained Mrs. Byrnes. "She is a brave, clever girl who manages to end the battle between the soldiers and the Indians."

Collette felt an instant liking for Hannah. What a smart little girl she must have been to create friends out of enemies.

"Collette," whispered Sarah from across the aisle, "which part do you want?"

Collette shrugged, trying to look puzzled. She felt funny admitting to Sarah that she suddenly wanted to be Hannah. It wasn't because it was the lead, it was because she really liked Hannah.

But more than liking Hannah, Collette wanted to share the same project with Sarah. After all, friends were supposed to stick together, no matter what.

Mrs. Byrnes put on her reading glasses and got out a notebook and a red pen.

"All right now. Would anybody like to go first?"

Twenty-five hands shot up like rockets.

Mrs. Byrnes laughed. "Well, I'm glad to have such an enthusiastic cast." She picked ten children to audition first.

Collette closed her eyes, thinking what a wonderful play it would be. Sarah and she could paint great scenery on the large brown paper kept in the art room. They'd paint trees with little bird nests, and maybe a rainbow to pin to the curtain. . . .

"Thank you," said Mrs. Byrnes after the first group had read. She used a brisk, no-nonsense voice so nobody could tell if they had gotten the part or not.

"Next, let's have Marsha reading for Hannah. . . . Roger will read for Mr. Johnson. . . . Sarah can read for Elise," continued Mrs. Byrnes.

Collette was glad she wasn't picked to read yet. She wanted to really concentrate on how good Marsha and Sarah would be.

She leaned forward in her seat, listening as her two friends pretended to be someone else. Collette could tell Marsha was really nervous. Her voice sounded high and extra-loud, as though she was about to start screaming any minute. But her arm movements were great. She threw out a hand, or pounded on a desk top with each sentence. Sarah read her lines clearly, smiling out at the class when she finished. She gave a slight curtsy and sat back in her seat. She was breathless, as though she had just run the length of the gym and back.

Marsha stared a hole right through Mrs. Byrnes's notebook. She was probably trying to see what her teacher had written about her audition.

Next, Collette was asked to read for the part of Hannah.

Marsha spun around in her seat and shot Collette an angry look.

Collette reached for the script and began reading. She forgot all about Marsha scowling at her. It was easy to pretend she was Hannah. Hannah said the same things Collette would have said.

" 'There will be no feast this year. The Indians will just raid our celebration,' " read William.

Collette cleared her throat. " 'Let's make this celebration one we will always remember. Let's invite the Indians. It could be the start of a friendship.' "

" 'You speak like a child,' " roared William.

" 'I am a child. And if I must remain a child to see things clearly, I will. We have been at war too long. It is time for peace. If it needs to begin with me, then it shall begin with me.' "

"Thank you, children," said Mrs. Byrnes. She closed her notebook.

Collette continued to leaf through the script. She wondered what Hannah would do to get the Indians and soldiers together.

The rest of the day passed quickly. Everyone was waiting for dismissal. That was when Mrs. Byrnes was going to pass out the scripts again. Only this time, the name of the character would be printed on top.

The large white clock ticked away. The bell finally rang.

Collette, Marsha, and Sarah huddled together in a nervous knot. ·

"I may just faint," whispered Marsha.

Collette patted Marsha's arm. "You did a wonderful job, Marsha. I bet you got the part. And even if you didn't, you can always help Sarah and me with the scenery."

"My mom will take us out to lunch and everything," added Sarah. "I don't think our dads will mind if we borrow a few of their old shirts to paint in."

"Girls, pick up your scripts," called Mrs. Byrnes.

Marsha dashed across the floor, grabbing the script from Mrs. Byrnes's hand.

"Louise!" shrieked Marsha. "I . . . I don't believe it. I didn't want the part of Louise!"

Sarah reached for her script.

"I'm Mrs. Hudson. . . . Oh no! I wonder who my husband is?"

Roger slid up beside her and wiggled his eyebrows.

"What's for dinner tonight, honey?"

"Gross!" cried Sarah as she turned away. "I want a divorce!"

Collette laughed, wondering if she had to be married to anyone.

"Who are you, Collette?" asked Sarah. "I hope you're married to someone, too."

Collette looked down at her script. Her mouth fell open as she quickly folded the script in half.

"My mother is going to be so disappointed," moaned Marsha. "She may not even come if I only have ten lines. Boy-oh-boy, this is the story of my aunt all over again."

"Collette, let me see," asked Sarah, trying to reach for the script.

Collette tried to hold tightly to her script. She wanted to tell Sarah and Marsha herself . . . later.

"What?" said Sarah loudly. "I don't believe it."

Marsha grabbed the script.

"Let me see!"

"What! Hannah! There has to be some sort of a mistake!"

"I didn't ask to read for Hannah . . ." whispered Collette. "Mrs. Byrnes told me to."

Marsha pushed her face closer to Collette's.

"But you did, didn't you? You could have just said no."

Collette stared at her script.

Sarah walked past her and picked up her book bag.

"I guess this means we won't be painting scenery together, Collette."

Marsha tossed her script inside her desk and slammed the lid shut. "Well, let's go to our lockers, Sarah. I guess this day is over."

Sarah and Marsha walked out the door, side by side. Collette frowned as Sarah patted Marsha on the back.

Collette felt tears stinging. Her entire chest hurt, a sure sign that her heart was breaking into a million pieces.

It wasn't her fault that Mrs. Byrnes gave her the lead role. She could understand Marsha being mean to her; she did it lots of times.

But why was Sarah treating her like this?

Other children came to congratulate Collette on getting the part of Hannah. But it wasn't enough.

She watched as Marsha and Sarah came back in the room. They leaned against the blackboard, waiting for buses to be called. They whispered, laughed, the two of them huddling close together and leaving Collette out.

They were probably deciding to become best friends.

And that meant she was going to stay on the outside forever, without any best friend at all.

Chapter Eight

Collette dreaded the bus ride to school Friday morning. She knew Marsha would totally ignore her, which she did.

As Collette walked down the aisle of the bus, Marsha plopped her book bag on the seat beside her. That was an unwritten law that Collette better not try to share a seat with her.

Collette looked around the bus. Now what was she supposed to do? She always sat with Marsha, every morning.

"Hey, Collette," called Jeff from the middle of the bus.

As Collette walked down the aisle, Jeff moved over, squeezing his friend Keto against the window.

"You can sit with us until Marsha starts missing you being her friend," said Jeff.

Collette tried to only take up a little of the seat.

"Yeah, then you won't have to sit with us," added Keto as he wiggled around, looking for more room.

Collette couldn't help but smile. It was nice to have a part of your family on the bus, after all.

Last night at dinner, Collette had told her family that she had the lead in the Christmas play.

"Wonderful," said Daddy.

"Not wonderful," said Collette. "I don't want the part of Hannah. I just wanted to have a little part and paint scenery with Sarah."

"You're just nervous," said Mother soothingly. "I'll help you with your lines."

"It will be a wonderful experience for you," added Daddy.

"A wonderful experience where I can end up losing all of my friends," cried Collette. Her voice was beginning to wiggle, and she could feel the tears, just waiting to fall.

"Friends, good friends, would be happy for you getting the lead," said Daddy gently. "Good friends are like family."

Collette frowned as she remembered her father's words.

Good friends are like family.

It wasn't true. It wasn't a bit true for Collette. Sometimes family, especially little brothers and sisters, ruined things. Good friends were supposed to make everything extra special.

As soon as the bus stopped, Collette hopped off and went right into the building. She didn't want to wait around for Sarah to ignore her, too.

She wanted to talk to Mrs. Byrnes right away. She wanted to give her back the lead in the play before it could do serious damage to her friendship with Sarah and Marsha. Especially with Sarah. She had waited eight years to have a best friend, and she wasn't about to trade her in for the lead in the Christmas play.

Besides, Megan Brookes's slumber party was tomorrow night. She couldn't stand the thought of Marsha and Sarah palling around together.

Collette went inside the building and walked quickly down the hall and into the classroom. She was glad to find Mrs. Byrnes in the room alone.

Mrs. Byrnes stood on a chair, stapling colorful turkeys around the border of the bulletin board.

"Good morning, Collette. You're just in time to hand me a few turkeys."

Collette held up a handful. "I wanted to talk to you about the play."

Mrs. Byrnes smiled. "I think this is going to be the best Christmas play the school's ever done."

Collette nodded. "Yes, I think so, too. But . . . well, you see . . . I forgot to tell you that I'm real busy with piano and art lessons. Plus, you know my mom has a lot of kids so I help her after school. . . ."

Mrs. Byrnes gave a puzzled smile.

"So, I won't be able to play Hannah," continued Collette in a rush. "I'll be too busy at home to learn all the lines. Loading the dishwasher, tying Stevie's shoes. . . ."

Mrs. Byrnes laughed a deep laugh. "You won't have a bit of trouble with the lines, Collette. You are absolutely perfect for the part."

Things weren't going as smoothly as Collette had hoped. She thought Mrs. Byrnes would just say okay and let her off the hook.

"Painting scenery would be good for me," suggested Collette. "You can give my part away to another girl. Lots of girls want the part."

Mrs. Byrnes took off her glasses and looked at Collette.

"Is something wrong, Collette?"

Collette tried her best to look carefree.

"No. I'm just really busy. I don't want the lead in the play."

Collette stared at the turkeys lying on the desk. Once the words came out, they sounded pretty rude.

"Are you turning the part down because some of the other children might feel envious?" asked Mrs. Byrnes in a low, gentle voice.

Collette wasn't quite sure, but it sounded like something she was probably doing.

"Would it be all right if I just painted scenery?"

Mrs. Byrnes put on her glasses and sighed.

"Yes, Collette . . . if you're sure that's what you want. I'll give your part to another girl in the class."

Collette picked up her book bag and looked around the class. Maybe she should offer to water the plants, or fix up the bookshelves. Something to let Mrs. Byrnes know that she really liked having her as a teacher.

But Mrs. Byrnes stood up, tucking the extra

turkeys under her arm as she climbed back onto the chair. She didn't need Collette's help.

Collette walked back out on the playground. She could hardly wait to tell Sarah the good news. Marsha and Sarah were leaning against the bike rack.

"Hi," said Collette. "I was in talking to Mrs. Byrnes about the play."

Marsha gave a slight scowl, but Sarah nodded.

"Are we going to have rehearsal today?"

"She didn't say. I went in to tell her that I didn't want to be Hannah. I want to paint scenery, just like we planned, Sarah."

Marsha suddenly came to life. She grabbed Collette's arm excitedly.

"Did you ask her to give the part to me?"

"Was Mrs. Byrnes mad at you when you told her?" asked Sarah.

"No." Collette shook Marsha away and smiled at Sarah. She really was a good friend to worry.

"Great! Now the two of us can paint scenery," said Sarah. "My mom said that she'll find some old shirts of my dad's. Things will be just as we planned."

"I will just roll into a ball and die if I don't get

91

the part of Hannah," whined Marsha. "I just can't lose out on it twice."

The morning bell sounded, herding the children toward the door.

"I'm going to have a little talk with Mrs. Byrnes," shouted Marsha over her shoulder. "I better let her know that I am willing to trade in my old part in the play."

"Why don't you come over to my house after school and we can draw some plans for the scenery?" suggested Sarah. "Maybe you can stay for dinner."

"Great," said Collette. Suddenly she felt so happy she could burst.

She thought of her father saying that friends were like family. He was wrong! Family could never make her feel this happy.

Giving up the part of Hannah to paint scenery with Sarah was a terrific idea.

When Collette and Sarah walked into the classroom, they started to giggle. Marsha was waving the script in front of Mrs. Byrnes, hopping from foot to foot as she tried to snatch the part of Hannah.

"Sit down, children," called Mrs. Byrnes as

she walked over to close the door. "I have an announcement."

Marsha's grin widened an extra foot as she slid into her chair. She turned and winked at Collette, raising her arms in a victory sign.

"The role of Hannah was returned to me," announced Mrs. Byrnes.

A groan of pure disbelief whizzed through the room, eyes darting as they tried to figure out why Collette would be so dumb as to pass up the lead in the Christmas play.

"And so," continued Mrs. Byrnes as she flipped through her tiny notebook, "after rechecking my notes from yesterday's auditions, I have reassigned the role to Sarah Messland."

"Sarah!" cried Marsha, half rising from her seat.

"Sarah!" whispered Collette.

Turning in her seat, she watched Sarah's face darken to a bright pink.

Oh no, thought Collette. This was just too awful for poor Mrs. Byrnes. She was going to feel terrible when Sarah turned down the part, too. Her feelings would be positively smashed.

"Can you help me out, Sarah?" asked Mrs. Byrnes.

Poor Sarah. It was going to be even harder for her to turn down the role. She had to stand up and refuse it in front of the whole class.

Collette sighed, wishing there was something she could do to help Sarah. She smiled. Maybe Sarah would be less nervous if she saw her good friend sitting there with a big smile on her face.

Sarah stood up.

"Yes, I'd love to!"

Collette slumped back in her seat, deflating by the second as she stared at Sarah.

She'd love it? Love it? How could Sarah love being Hannah? Hannah was the part her best friend had just returned.

Didn't Sarah realize that she couldn't paint scenery if she had the lead?

Marsha put her head down on her desk. She was so deep into her bad luck that she didn't budge.

Maybe Sarah was just too embarrassed to refuse it with the whole class listening. She would probably wait until she got Mrs. Brynes alone and then explain things.

Mrs. Byrnes bent down and wrote HANNAH in big block letters on the top of Sarah's script.

Then she walked down Collette's aisle. She stopped and scratched out the name HANNAH.

It only took one smooth stroke to wipe it all away.

"You may have Sarah's old part," Mrs. Byrnes said quietly. "Mrs. Hudson."

Collette sat and waited. She waited all through rehearsal for Sarah to talk to Mrs. Byrnes. She waited for her to raise her hand and tell the whole class that she would rather paint scenery with her very best friend, Collette, than play the lead.

She sat and waited all morning for Sarah to return the part of Hannah. But she never did.

In the cafeteria, Sarah squeezed in between Marsha and Collette, acting as if nothing had changed.

"We are going to have so much fun at Megan's slumber party tonight. Maybe my mom could — "

Collette couldn't wait any longer.

"Why did you take the part of Hannah?" she blurted out.

Marsha and Sarah both looked at each other, raising their eyebrows as if they thought Collette was awfully rude to even ask.

"Collette, what was I supposed to do? You know how shy I am. I couldn't stand up there and tell the whole class that I didn't want the part either."

"Yeah," added Marsha. "Mrs. Byrnes probably thinks no one even wants to do her stupid play."

Collette pushed her sandwich out of the way.

"But the whole reason I gave the part of Hannah back was so we could paint scenery together, Sarah."

Sarah's face got red. She pretended she was real interested in opening her orange drink carton.

"I know. But what if I give the part back and Mrs. Byrnes just cancels the play? Then the whole class would hate me." Sarah tried to smile at Collette. "You can ask somebody else. I can't draw as well as you, anyway."

Marsha took an angry bite out of her sandwich.

"I can't believe Mrs. Byrnes chose you over me, Sarah. I told her all about my aunt and everything. You would think she would want to take advantage of hometown talent."

Collette played with her sandwich, taking small bites that were still too big for her to swallow.

The hard lump in her throat wouldn't let anything past. And now that Sarah refused to give the role of Hannah back, the lump would continue to grow.

"Maybe if I went with you to talk to her . . ." began Collette.

"Oh, forget about it," grumbled Marsha. "It's too late. Stop being a crybaby about it."

"I'm not," hissed Collette. She was getting too mad to cry. Sarah wasn't any different than Marsha, not really.

The two of them deserved to have each other for a best friend. Let them spend the rest of their lives being mean to each other.

Collette stood, shoving everything into her lunchbox. She could hardly wait to go to Megan's party tonight. She would laugh and eat popcorn and have so much fun looking for a new best friend.

And when she did find her she would be fair and nice to her. She would be loyal and kind and never double-cross her.

Tonight at the party she would have the best time of her life. She would show Sarah how wrong she had been to trade her in for Hannah.

Chapter Nine

"Can I come to the party?" asked Laura. She handed Collette her slippers to add to the overnight bag. "I'll be good."

"No. Megan just asked me. She doesn't even know you, Laura."

Laura crawled into her bunk bed and pulled the covers up under her chin.

"What if I have a nightmare without you here? Maybe you could ask the girls to have the party at your house, instead."

Collette shuddered at the thought. She'd never have a slumber party at her house. There were definitely too many Murphys racing around, acting crazy, making noise, crying when they couldn't find a toy.

Going to Megan's house would be fun. Megan was practically an only child. She just had an older teenage sister who practically never came out of her room.

Maybe Megan would be a good choice for her new best friend. Megan was real nice to everyone at school. She always picked Collette to be on her team when she was made captain in gym class.

Collette added her toothbrush and comb.

No, maybe not Megan. She was nice, but she liked to watch TV too much, even when friends came over.

Collette needed someone who liked to play school and pretend they were stranded on a tiny island with the sand eroding away a little more each day. . . . Someone who would wrap a beach towel around themselves and call it a Cinderella ball gown and not feel silly. . . .

Someone like Sarah.

"I wrote you a little note and put it under your pillow, all right, Laura?" Collette lifted her bag and started to walk to the stairs. "Have Mommy read it to you before you go to bed and you'll have a good dream."

Laura threw back the covers and hopped out of bed, giving Collette a hug.

"Thanks, Collette. You are a great sister, all right."

Collette hugged Laura back, glad that someone still thought she was great.

"Ready to go?" asked Daddy from the hall. "Your present is already wrapped. I put it on the kitchen table."

"Thanks," said Collette, handing him her bag.

"Are we picking up Marsha and Sarah?" asked Daddy.

Collette shook her head. She didn't tell her parents about Sarah taking the role of Hannah. They were already upset that she gave up the role.

Telling them Sarah took the part, quick as a wink, would probably make them mad at Sarah, too.

It would be awful if Collette's parents called Sarah's and demanded that she give the role of Hannah back to Collette.

The whole school would take sides, some of them wanting Collette, some of them wanting Sarah.

"No," she said finally. "Marsha ate dinner at Sarah's house. They'll ride over together, I guess."

"Have a good time tonight," said Daddy. He put his hand on Collette's shoulder as they walked down the stairs. "Make sure you dream about your dad, okay?"

Collette laughed. Her dad was so corny. He was always telling her things like that.

"Don't worry about the play, either," added Dad. "You are such a good artist, you should be painting the scenery."

Collette nodded, not trusting her voice. She was pretty good at art. But she knew deep down that she would have been a pretty good Hannah.

She suddenly remembered a rule her mother had. She said it was fine to give away toys or trade them for others with your friends. But you had to think it out first, because she didn't allow Indian-givers. What you gave away, you weren't allowed to ask for back, just because you changed your mind.

Collette went into the kitchen and kissed her mom.

" 'Bye, see you at eleven tomorrow."

Mother hugged her.

" 'Bye, honey. Give us a call if you get too tired to last all night."

The night air chilled Collette as soon as she opened the door. She wasn't even in the car, and she already felt a little homesick.

Maybe she shouldn't go after all.

Sarah and Marsha would be palling around together, showing off that they were best friends. Maybe everyone at the whole party would be standing around with a best friend, leaving Collette with nobody but herself. She'd probably just watch TV with Megan's parents upstairs. They'd feel real sorry for her and make Megan pretend to be her friend.

"Dad, maybe I should stay home," said Collette quickly as she stopped by the car. "Laura is afraid that she will have nightmares without me in the room, and you know how Mommy hates for me to stay up late, eating junk food and. . . ."

Daddy looked so concerned, Collette almost cried.

"You don't have to go, Peanut."

Collette swallowed, hating that lump that wouldn't go away.

She did have to go. If she didn't, Marsha would blab stories about her, saying she didn't come because Sarah took the part of Hannah, and wasn't she a big crybaby.

Collette shook her head, smiling a fake smile.

"No, I'll go. I guess I was just worried about Laura."

Daddy slid in under the steering wheel and unlocked Collette's door.

"You're a good sister, Collette. No wonder Laura loves you so much."

Daddy put the key in the ignition and laughed.

"Laura told me that you are her best friend in the whole world."

Collette smiled, nodding her head as she stared out the window.

That was a good thing to remember. Because if she couldn't find someone special tonight at the party, she might just have to settle for her four-year-old sister as a best friend for the rest of her life.

Chapter Ten

It was Marsha's idea for the ginger-ale-gulping contest. She convinced everyone at the slumber party that teenagers played this game at their parties all the time.

"Now when I give the signal, everyone drink their ginger ale as fast as they can," explained Marsha. "You're not allowed to stop. The first one finished will be the winner."

Collette knew that Marsha was in a great mood because she was in charge. She got to tell a whole room full of girls what to do.

Collette listened to the signal and then took a big gulp. She covered her mouth and tried to swallow. The bubbles burned her throat and started to crawl up the inside of her nose.

She didn't want to ruin her nose, just to be polite. She set her can of ginger ale down and watched the others.

Kathy and Jody were doing pretty well. They were both nice girls. Collette had sat next to them during pizza. They were friendly, and for a while Collette was sure that they would make great new best friends. But then they both started talking about things they had done together, like sleeping over at each other's houses and making Christmas cookies together every year.

Collette had felt so lonely and sad, knowing that she was going to have to start all over again with someone, making new memories from scratch.

"I won, I won," shouted Marsha as she raced around the room, holding her can of ginger ale high in the air.

Collette smiled. Marsha had probably practiced gulping for hours at home, just so she would win.

No one had much time to congratulate Marsha. Allison burped and then threw up real fast. Jody jumped back so she wouldn't get splashed on and knocked over the dip bowl, right on the rug.

Megan started to yell and her mother came running in.

Collette wasn't surprised when Megan's mother announced that as soon as she cleaned up the disgusting mess, it would be time for "lights out."

Everyone moaned and groaned, but mostly they ran for their sleeping bags. Collette was glad that a strict mother lived there so everyone would finally settle down and go to sleep.

Not that she had anyone picked out for a best friend, somebody who would want her to put her sleeping bag down next to them.

She had looked and looked during the whole party. She played cards with Lorraine. Things were going fine till Lorraine lost at War and started to whimper. She said she had a headache and quit in the middle of the next game.

At dinner she had tried out Kathy. But Kathy sat and picked everything, including the cheese, from her pizza. She piled it in a messy heap on her napkin.

Even though Collette was used to eating with Stevie every day, she still wasn't used to anyone destroying food like that. She couldn't pick Kathy for a best friend; she'd never be able to sit next to her in the cafeteria for lunch.

Collette sighed, unrolling her sleeping bag. She

dragged it back beside the couch. She could just sleep here by herself. She'd go to sleep and then it would be morning and she could go home.

"Is this spot saved?"

Collette looked up and saw Sarah standing there, looking embarrassed.

"No, go ahead," said Collette, very politely.

"Thanks," said Sarah, just as politely.

They were both pretending that nothing had happened, that things were exactly the same.

But they both knew that something had changed the best-friendness between them.

Hannah had bored tiny holes into their friendship, letting all the specialness seep right out through the holes.

"Make room, make room!" shouted Marsha. She dragged her bright green sleeping bag across the floor with one hand and shoved a handful of potato chips into her mouth with the other.

Of course, Marsha didn't even bother to ask if it was all right to sleep next to them. She just took it for granted that everyone wanted her around.

In a way, Collette was glad that Marsha was there. Since she was always talking or complaining about something, the silence between Collette and Sarah didn't seem so silent.

Megan's mom flipped the lights on and off a couple of times, then the room was dark.

Someone gave a scary groan.

Marsha's flashlight went on immediately. She laid it next to her sleeping bag. "I'll be the monster patrol," she announced.

Everyone laughed, but Collette only smiled. She knew that Marsha was afraid of the dark.

Collette blinked sleepily. She sure wished Sarah was still her best friend so they could whisper together. Whispering in the dark was the best part of a slumber party.

In the darkness Collette listened jealously to the muffled giggles.

Collette reached for her can of ginger ale, taking a small sip before she set it on the coffee table near her.

She yawned, glad she would soon be asleep. In the darkness she stared at the glow from Marsha's flashlight. In the outer edge she could see Marsha's closed eyes.

Marsha and Sarah weren't whispering to each other, which made it easier to be next to them.

Collette would have cried if the two of them had shared secrets together all night.

Collette yawned again and closed her eyes, wondering if Laura was having a nice dream.

It seemed like only a minute later when sunlight hit her closed eyes. Collette blinked, rubbing her eyes as she sat up.

It was morning, early morning.

Sunlight, yellow and dust-filled, slid through the slats of the blinds from the window. She swallowed, frowning as she tasted last night's pizza.

As she reached for her can of ginger ale, she glanced over at Sarah. She was still asleep. Sarah's covers were kicked to the bottom of her unzipped sleeping bag.

Collette leaned closer and groaned. Oh, no! A large, dark stain rested underneath Sarah, darkening her pale blue sleeping bag.

Sarah had wet her sleeping bag.

Collette scrambled to her feet, clutching her ginger ale can and trying to think.

As soon as Marsha and the other girls woke up they would notice the wet stain and start laughing. Marsha would scream and yank her new sleeping bag quickly away. She wasn't really the type to stick by someone, even a new best friend.

Sarah needed someone to stick by her, right now.

But then, Sarah hadn't stuck by Collette very well when it came to Hannah. She didn't hand in the role and make plans to paint scenery.

As the sun rose higher, the stain stood out more. How could this have happened, anyway? Sarah had spent the night at her house at least four times, and never once did anything like this happen.

It must have been all the ginger ale they had last night.

Collette looked around the room. Several of the girls were beginning to yawn, stretching as they tried to climb out of their dreams.

Collette had to think fast. She couldn't let Sarah wake up to the sounds of everyone laughing at her; she just couldn't.

Sarah may not be her best friend right now, but when she was her best friend, she was the best there could be.

Sarah, still sound asleep, both hands shoved deep under her pillow, looked so unprotected.

Looking down at her, Collette remembered the

times Sarah would stick up for her when Marsha hurt her feelings, or how she would always remember to bring Collette a nice souvenir from trips she took. On every postcard she sent, Sarah would write *Wish you were here* and underline it four times.

Collette felt a prickle of guilt race up her arms. Maybe she shouldn't have blamed Sarah so much for taking Hannah. After all, Sarah had never even once asked her to give it up.

Marsha flopped over on her back and started to yawn noisily. Any minute now she would open her eyes and look around the room. Any minute now she would discover Sarah's secret.

Collette leaned closer and started to empty her can of ginger ale up and down on top of Sarah and the sleeping bag. The ginger ale bubbled and splattered, causing Sarah to bolt upright like a jackrabbit.

"What!" she shrieked. "Holy cow, Collette! What are you doing?"

Collette helped Sarah to stand, quickly handing her her own robe.

"Here — put this on. I'm sorry, Sarah. I got you all wet. I can't believe how clumsy I am. I started to drink my ginger ale and it just. . . . just slipped right out of my hands."

"My nightgown's soaked!" wailed Sarah, wrapping the robe tightly around her. "I'm freezing!"

"Who has the megamouth?" demanded Marsha. She sat up, saw the mess, and quickly scooted away. "What happened?"

Collette opened her mouth to reexplain, but stopped when she saw the frightened look on Sarah's face. She was wide awake now, staring at her sleeping bag. She gripped the robe more tightly around herself and shivered. Collette could tell that Sarah knew exactly what had happened.

"I spilled a whole can of ginger ale all over Sarah," said Collette quickly. She forced herself to giggle like it was all a big joke.

Marsha untangled herself from her covers and stood up. She shoved her hands on her hips and frowned at Collette.

"Well, aren't you the funny guy? Sarah and I don't think it's a bit cute. And don't you think for a minute that we believe all this was an accident, Collette. You're still mad about Hannah!"

"She is not. Leave her alone, Marsha!" shouted Sarah.

112

The room was silent, as the rest of the girls waited to hear what was going to happen next.

Collette shrugged. She wasn't about to tell Marsha a thing.

Marsha took a protective step closer to Sarah.

Sarah looked at Collette, her face getting redder all the time. She looked like she was ready to cry.

"I said it was an accident, and it was," said Collette softly. She really only wanted Sarah to hear.

Sarah reached out and put her hand on Collette's arm.

"Of course it was, Collette. I know that."

"What?" shouted Marsha. She looked very disappointed. "She ruined your new sleeping bag, Sarah! Don't tell me you're not mad about that!"

Sarah bent down and started to fold her wet bag into a tight roll.

"It was an accident. I bumped into Collette, and she spilled her ginger ale." Sarah looked up and smiled at Collette. "We're both clumsy!"

Marsha sighed and grabbed her robe.

"Doughnuts!" cried Megan from the doorway. "Come and get it!"

Marsha hopped across the sleeping bags, her

robe flapping like wings as she flew across the floor.

"Hungry this morning, isn't she?" giggled Collette. She bent down and helped Sarah tie the ends of the sleeping bag.

"I'll drop your robe off later," said Sarah slowly. "My mom . . . will . . . you know, wash it and everything.

Collette nodded. She didn't think Sarah had to explain a thing, not even to her.

"Thanks, Collette."

Collette looked up. She could tell by Sarah's shaky voice that she was thanking her for more than helping with the sleeping bag ties.

"That's what friends are for," said Collette quickly.

"Best friends, anyway," said Sarah, just as quickly.

Collette nodded, and then they both started to laugh. Collette looked at her watch, glad she still had two more hours before her dad came to pick her up.

It was finally starting to feel like a party.

Chapter Eleven

Collette raced into the house, swinging her overnight bag back and forth like a pendulum. She and Sarah were best friends again and the whole world looked as happy as she felt.

"Hi there, honey," said Mother. She laughed as Collette gave her an extra-tight hug. "It must have been a good party."

"Hi. I had such a good time. Sarah is going to call me later, Mommy. She wants to know if I can go to Florida with her family over Christmas."

Mother looked a little surprised.

"Well, that's awfully nice of her to ask, Collette. Maybe when you're older."

"But she wants me to go. Her parents — "

"Can I go to Florida?" asked Jeff. "I want to see Disney World."

"Me, too," said Laura. "I am going to put it down on my Christmas list."

"Can I go?" asked Collette. "I've never been to Florida. Sarah goes every year."

"Sarah is an only child," said Mother. She stepped across Stevie, who was coloring on the floor. "Stevie, can you sit at the table and color?"

"He needs me to help him spell words," said Jeff. He leaned against the leg of the kitchen table.

"You better make your Christmas list, Collette," said Stevie. "Santa needs time to make toys."

Collette let her overnight bag fall to the ground.

"I don't want toys. I want to go to Florida with Sarah."

"Not at Christmastime," said Mother. "Christmas is a time for family."

"Yeah," said Jeff. "You have to stick around so you can buy me a present."

"Sarah and I just got to be best friends again," whined Collette. Maybe if she could make her mom understand how important it was for her to be with Sarah, she would change her mind.

"Invite Sarah over this afternoon," suggested Mother, pulling out a tray of cookies. "Hey, look at these cookies. I'm really getting good at this baking stuff."

"But I want to go on a trip with her," continued Collette. "If you won't let *me* go to Florida with her, then can our whole family go to Florida? We could stay in the same hotel with the Messlands, and. . . ."

Mother laughed and shook her head.

"No way. It would cost too much money to take a family of six to Florida."

"But Sarah goes every year!" protested Collette.

"Sarah has more money 'cause she's an only child, right, Mom?" said Jeff.

"Right," said Mother. "But I wouldn't trade you guys for a million dollars."

Everyone laughed. Mother bent down and passed the cookies.

Collette shook her head to the cookies, shaking it even harder when she thought about everything she was going to miss out on. Sarah would probably call Marsha and ask her to go. Marsha's parents would suggest that they all go together, rent a condominium, maybe fly down in a private jet.

For a family of six, it was too expensive to do anything fun.

"Maybe we can start a special fund and go to Disney World in a year or two," suggested Mother. "Stevie would be big enough to go on all the rides."

"A year or two?" wailed Collette. "I'll be too big to go on any of the rides. Everyone in the whole world has already been there but us!"

"You're exaggerating," said Mother. Her voice was beginning to sound a little worn out.

"Here's my list!" cried Stevie.

Mother studied the wrinkled paper, filled with circles and smudges.

"Well, it sure looks like everything is here, Stevie. Santa will be happy to get this."

Stevie walked over and leaned against Collette.

"I'll help you with your list now, Collette," he offered. "I can color real good."

Collette frowned, staring out at the snowflakes batting themselves against the windows.

"No, thanks, Stevie. Santa won't be able to bring me what I really want."

Laura stood up, looking worried.

"But, Collette, you have to make a list. Santa will think you don't like his toys."

"Ask Santa for a dog," suggested Jeff. "A big one."

"No," said Collette shortly. She stood up and walked out of the kitchen. Nobody understood how crowded she felt at times. She couldn't even refuse to make a stupid Christmas list without everyone in the whole family butting in and telling her what to do.

Stevie followed her out of the kitchen, smiling and holding a fat purple marker up in his hand like a torch.

"You better make a list or I'll color your leg, Collette."

Collette frowned, crossing her arms and watching as everyone, even her own mother, started to laugh.

"Get away from me, Stevie," said Collette, giving him a push. "This house is so . . . noisy. I bet our neighbors think we live in a . . . a zoo!"

"Yeah," laughed Jeff, pointing to Collette. "And you're the monkey."

Collette was so mad she wanted to scream. She

didn't think they were funny. They were awful.

"Maybe I should make a Christmas list after all," she sputtered, walking back into the room. "And I would only ask for one thing."

Everyone was watching her now, waiting to hear what she would ask for.

"I'd ask to be an only child . . . just like Sarah and Marsha. Nobody laughs at them. They get to do fun things and go fun places."

"You don't mean that," said Mother. She was watching Collette with a real disappointed look on her face, as if Collette had just announced that she enjoyed stealing candy from the drugstore.

"I do," insisted Collette, knowing her mother wouldn't like to hear her say it again. "I mean it."

The kitchen seemed to sink in silence, everyone frozen as they watched Collette.

"Don't you like us anymore, Collette?" asked Laura finally. She leaned against Mother and started to suck her thumb.

"Of course she does," said Mother quickly. "She's tired, that's all."

Collette could feel the tears on her cheeks, so she had to be crying. But she didn't know if she was sad because she was lying about her wish, or if she was crying because she was telling the truth.

She hurried down the hall and sat on the bottom step, waiting for someone to come and comfort her.

But nobody came with a cup of tea to cheer her up, or a cool hand for her head.

They all had each other in the kitchen; nobody even noticed that one less Murphy was in the room.

With both hands, Collette wiped away her tears. As she looked over her shoulder, she could see her mother watching her from the doorway.

She was probably thinking how awful it was to have such a selfish little girl who wanted to wish away her brothers and a sweet little sister.

Just so she could go to Disney World. Just so she could have a quiet house.

Collette sighed. Why couldn't she wish for something simple like a fluffy cat or a doll that would talk and walk.

Now her Christmas wishes just got her in trouble.

Chapter Twelve

"My wish came true!" cried Laura. "Collette, wake up and look!"

Collette rolled over and yawned. Laura was standing on her little green stool, pointing at the snowstorm outside the bedroom window.

"What wish?" asked Collette.

"I asked Santa to bring me a snowflake shower. No thunder, no rain, just snow!"

Collette smiled, digging deeper into her covers.

Laura hopped from the stool, running to the closet and pulling down her sweater.

"Let's go outside and play in my wish, Collette."

"In a minute," she mumbled.

Laura already got a wish and Christmas was still a week away. She would probably end up getting everything she had asked for. A four-year-old's list was real easy to fill.

"Telegram!" shouted Jeff as he barged into the room. He walked over to Collette's bunk and tossed up an envelope. "Laura, hurry up and get dressed. Gramma is on her way over to pick us up. She's baby-sitting."

"Good," said Laura, stepping into her jeans. "I want to help her hang her candy canes on her porch, for the elves."

"Oh, great," moaned Collette. Every time she went to Gramma's without her parents, she was expected to keep an eye on Stevie. Gramma had china everywhere, and Stevie wanted to pick up everything.

"Get dressed, Collette," ordered Jeff as he walked out.

Collette threw back the blankets, put on her robe, and stared at the envelope. Jeff had probably written her a letter telling her how mean she was to want to be an only child.

Collette rammed the letter into the pocket of her robe and climbed down the ladder. She wanted to go down and see if she had to watch Stevie all afternoon.

This weekend was off to a real boring start.

"Look at my new boots," laughed Stevie as he marched down the hall.

Collette smiled. She had already worn the red and white boots. So had Jeff and Laura. But Stevie was so proud of them, not even caring that they were hand-me-downs.

"Hurry up, kids," called Daddy from the bottom of the stairwell. "Gramma is on her way!"

Collette hurried down, her hand brushing against the plastic green boughs Mother had wrapped around the banister. Little red bows were scattered among the green.

"Daddy, how long do we have to stay?" asked Collette. She loved Gramma, but she really was not in the mood to be a midget mother for Stevie all afternoon.

"Out of my way," shouted Jeff as he and Stevie clomped down the stairs. "Make way for the ski patrol men."

"Daddy, tie my hat," called Laura.

Collette stepped out of the way and waited until the little guys rushed past.

"Good morning, sleepyhead," said Mother. She reached out and gave Collette a hug. "Did you see all that snow? We're going to get a good two inches more this afternoon."

"Ya-hoo!" sang out Stevie. "I have my tough boots on to step on that snow."

"You're not even dressed yet, Collette," said Jeff. "Gramma's coming."

Mother handed Jeff his scarf and mittens.

"Don't worry, Jeff. Collette will see you guys later."

"Was she bad?" asked Laura.

"Of course not," said Daddy, trying to fit Stevie's thumb into his mitten.

Collette pulled her robe around her, wondering what she was supposed to do this afternoon. She hoped she didn't have to get a shot or her teeth cleaned.

The letter inside her pocket jabbed her. Reaching inside, Collette pulled it out.

"Gramma!" shouted Jeff from the doorway.

Daddy swung the door open, snowflakes blowing in as Jeff, Laura, and Stevie raced out.

Collette shivered, running to the window to wave to Gramma. Gramma looked up, red-faced and excited, as the three children surrounded her.

Collette waved again, looking down at the letter.

Her named had been printed in neat letters. Jeff couldn't print that neatly. Maybe it wasn't from him after all.

Flipping the letter over, Collette smiled. The return address was marked NORTH POLE.

As Gramma's car backed slowly out of the drive, Collette sat in the window seat and carefully opened the letter. Her mother was probably teasing her. She probably wrote this, pretending to be an elf, asking what Collette wanted for Christmas.

Collette skimmed the letter, then stood up and read it aloud:

CONGRATULATIONS!
YOUR CHRISTMAS WISH
IS ABOUT TO COME TRUE!
FOR THE NEXT 12 HOURS
YOU WILL BE TREATED TO
THE LIFE OF AN ONLY CHILD!
LOVE, SANTA

"Anything interesting in the mail?" joked Daddy.

Collette turned and hugged her father.

"I can't believe it. I'm really going to be an only child!"

"For twelve hours, Collette," laughed Mother. "Your brothers and sisters are not library books. We can't return them every time they get in the way."

Collette blushed.

Twelve hours . . . almost a whole day! They could all go to Station Square and walk into any store they wanted. No one had to worry about breaking things, or getting tired, or needing a bathroom . . . fast!

They could all go out to lunch, and they wouldn't have to go for fast food. They could go to a fancy place with soft music and real silverware.

"What should we do first?" asked Daddy. "Let's not waste a minute just standing around."

Collette nodded. She was in a hurry to get started.

"Wait a minute," she said, running back up the stairs.

In a flash she was back, dressed and holding a folded square.

"I wrote this list last week, just in case my wish did come true."

Mother and Daddy drew closer as Collette unfolded her square and started to read.

"One. *Read science report.*"

"Didn't you read that to us last night?" asked Daddy. "Or was that Jeff reading his social studies?"

"Daddy!" giggled Collette. "That was me, but I didn't get a chance to finish reading it, remember? Stevie flushed his socks down the toilet and you both ran out of the room."

Mother groaned. "That's the last time I let Stevie help me with the laundry."

"Okay, let's listen to your report," insisted Daddy. "No interruptions allowed."

Collette cleared her throat and began. She was surprised how short it was, without the usual Murphy interruptions.

Collette got out her red pen and checked off *Read science report.*

"Now, the next thing on the list is . . . *Walk to drugstore and have a sundae.*"

Daddy looked out the window and shivered.

"It's snowing out there, Peanut."

128

Mother stood up and pulled Daddy to his feet.

"Come on, sir, we're not going to let a few snow-flakes slow us down."

On the way down to Marcus's Drugstore, the three of them linked arms, taking long steps as they sank their boots into the drifting snow.

Collette was anxious for cars to pass them, honking at the trio. She wished Marsha and Sarah would whiz past, waving and honking their sur-prise to find Collette sandwiched between her parents.

"Hey, who is this?" laughed Mr. Boyce as they entered the drugstore. "This can't be the Murphy family. There aren't enough of you. No one biting into the candy bars, no one blowing straw wrappers across the counter."

Collette felt a sudden surge of happiness; this was almost like a party.

"This is how our family started out, Mr. Boyce."

"I remember now, yeah, come to think of it, you still look like the Murphy family."

They all went to the back of the store, to sit on the red vinyl stools and order their sundaes.

Daddy let Collette add up the bill, giving her a dollar to spend on herself.

"Go ahead, buy yourself something. I figure I just saved five dollars by not bringing the other three. Jeff always orders a banana split, and Stevie spills his first two Cokes. . . ."

Collette bought herself some Chapstick, then jingled the change in her hand.

"I'll take three suckers," she said, watching as Mr. Boyce stuck them into her bag.

She could put them under the little guys' pillows, kind of like a treat.

As soon as they got home, Collette hung up her coat and got out her list. She checked off *Walk to drugstore*, and read *Make fudge*.

"Fudge," bellowed Daddy. "You didn't tell me I was going to gain five pounds in the next twelve hours!"

"Come on," said Collette, pulling him by the hand to the kitchen.

"Hey, look at this clean place," whistled Mother. "Nobody messed up this room, or broke a glass, or left the refrigerator open while we were gone."

Mother sank into a chair and put up her feet.

"I think I am beginning to like this only child business."

Collette smiled, but only a little. She wasn't

130

quite sure if her mother should be enjoying Collette's wish this much. She was sure the little guys would cry if they knew they weren't the least bit missed.

"Daddy and I will do all the work and you can read the directions," explained Collette, setting a box of fudge mix down in front of her mother.

When the fudge was finished, Daddy and Collette decided that they should be the official tasters.

Daddy said they should try at least three pieces to be sure that it was a perfect batch.

Collette pulled the bowl closer and grinned, glad that she got to lick it all herself.

As Mother cleaned the counter, Collette took six large pieces of fudge and wrapped them in foil. She shoved them to the back of the counter.

"Wait till the guys taste this," she said. "Jeff loves fudge!"

"Hey," said Daddy, reaching for the foil package. "We don't even have to tell the kids about the fudge. . . ."

"Daddy!" cried Collette, pushing it behind the cookie jar. "You don't want to gain five pounds, remember?"

Mother took their hands and led them out of the kitchen.

"How are we doing with the list?"

"I hope I get to take a nap," pleaded Daddy. "I don't remember being this busy with only one child."

Collette opened the closet and handed everyone their coat.

"Next, the museum, to see the Christmas tree display."

"Great," said Mother, handing her coat to Daddy to hold. "Jeff said his teacher told him they have a Civil War tree."

"Come on," said Collette, scanning her list as she raced down the hall.

She tugged at the door and shivered as the wind tried to push her back into the house.

Being an only child was so much fun. And she still had nine more hours to go!

Chapter Thirteen

Collette's feet gave out before her parents'. She slid onto the marble bench, melting like a pat of butter against the wall.

She had never spent so many hours at the museum. She saw gem displays and knights' armor that she never even knew existed. Usually Stevie or Laura would start complaining long before they were even out of the dinosaur room.

"Let's go see the watercolors," suggested Mother. Daddy nodded. They were both acting like they were on some sort of a field trip for adults.

"I loved the gem room," said Mother. "I have never made it to the quartz display. Last time Stevie leaned against the security glass and set off the alarm. The guard stared at us until we left."

"Can you believe we have been here almost three hours and no one has gotten lost, hungry, or mad?" Daddy shook his head like it was some sort of miracle.

Actually, Collette was starving. Since the little guys weren't with them, Mother had not packed her usual emergency bag filled with gum, pretzel sticks, and crackers.

"Hey, look at this," said Daddy. He stopped in front of a bulletin board. "The Christmas train display is already up. If we went today, we wouldn't have to listen to the other children complain about the long line. Last year I held Laura for hours."

"Remember how Stevie cried because he couldn't push that little girl on the mechanical swing?" reminded Mother. "He thought the whole village was really alive."

Collette laughed. Laura and Stevie pointed to everything they saw with happy looks on their faces. They leaned over the fence, peering into each lighted window to see if tiny people were inside.

"Hey, look who's over there!" said Mrs. Murphy. She raised her hand and waved. "Merry Christmas!"

"Sarah!" cried Collette happily. "Are you going to see the trains, too?"

Sarah nodded, smiling as broadly as Collette.

"We've been in line for forty minutes already," said Sarah's father in a tired voice. "Two bus loads of senior citizens are ahead of us."

The adults groaned.

"Maybe we should come back another time," suggested Mother. "The museum closes at five. It's already after four."

Daddy snapped his fingers. "I've got a great idea. Let's go home and set up our own Christmas trains!"

Collette's head flew up, her eyes meeting her dad's.

She couldn't be hearing straight.

Grandpa's trains? The Christmas trains that the whole family does together?

"I'll pop some corn, put on some Christmas music," suggested Mother, warming to the idea.

Sarah's mother pushed back her sweater, checking her watch. "Gosh, look at the time. I think we are going to leave now, too. I still have to pick up the dry cleaning before we leave for the trip. Come on, Sarah, button up."

"Dry cleaning," groaned Sarah. She looked pretty disappointed.

Daddy reached out and put his arm around Collette's shoulder.

"If our 'only child' thinks it's okay, Sarah is welcome to come with us."

Collette and Sarah reached out and grabbed each other's hands.

"Great!" they both said at once.

"Wonderful," added Daddy. "With two big helpers, and no little guys to get in the way, we'll have the whole train set up before dinner."

Mrs. Messland kissed Sarah and started to pull on her coat.

"Thanks for including Sarah. I'm afraid Vince and I are all thumbs when it comes to trains. Ours stay up in the attic, year after year."

"This is going to be fun," said Sarah. "Do you have a toy schoolhouse and everything?"

"We do if Laura didn't hide it," said Mother. "She hates to pack Christmas things away each year."

The four of them walked across the marble floor, buttoning up and thinking about the fun ahead.

"Jeff is so good at piecing the train track together," said Collette. "And Laura has such tiny fingers, she can set up the village people and they never fall down. . . ."

"This year you girls can do all that," said Mother brightly. "No one fighting over who gets to put the engine on the track first."

"No Stevie throwing the engine down the laundry chute," said Daddy. He still sounded mad.

"He thought it would be like a car wash," put in Collette. Stevie didn't do it to be mean.

Sarah laughed.

"Your house is so funny."

"Not tonight," pointed out Mother. "It will be perfect, absolutely perfect."

She reached out and patted Collette on the back. "And this year we will use real marshmallows in the hot chocolate, not popcorn," laughed Mother.

Sarah laughed.

"Laura doesn't like marshmallows because they melt too fast," explained Collette.

"We won't have to have the shredded wheat mountain this year either," continued Mother. "Jeff insisted that we use the whole box."

137

Daddy held the heavy wooden doors open and they walked outside.

It was almost dark now, the white flakes swirling in the shadows. Collette and Sarah shivered, shrinking back into their heavy coats.

"Let's pick up a pizza and get busy," suggested Daddy. He reached into his coat pocket and pulled out his car keys. He jingled them, humming "Jingle Bells."

"What a nice day," said Mother. She lifted her collar and looked up to study the snow. "Laura sure made a nice wish with this snow."

"The wish. . . . Wait a minute!" said Collette. She waved the snowflakes out of her way as she hurried to the lamp post. Reaching into her pocket she drew out the list. "Let me see what's next."

"Oh, no," groaned Daddy. "If you mention ice skating, I'm running in the other direction."

"Only one more thing on the list," laughed Collette as she bent down to study the paper.

Sarah stomped her feet, pulling her hat down over her forehead. "I can't believe you got to do a whole list of wishes, Collette. This is really great."

"I know," agreed Collette. "And I was saving the best till last."

Everyone drew a step closer, standing under the yellow circle of light splashed on the snowy sidewalk.

"We get into the car . . . drive across the bridge . . . and pick up the guys at Gramma's house."

"What?" shouted Daddy above the roar of a passing bus. "Let me see that list. That couldn't have been written by an only child."

Collette held the list up, laughing as she released it to the blustering gust of wind trailing the bus.

Collette watched as her paper tumbled and somersaulted, disappearing into the night.

"Let's go to Gramma's. We can all help with the trains," said Collette quietly. "Like always."

"Sounds like old times to me," said Mother. She reached out and linked arms with Daddy.

Collette leaned over and linked arms with Sarah. The two of them walked briskly up the sidewalk.

Up ahead, in the tiny parklet, tiny white lights flashed on, bringing the small blue spruce trees to life.

At the crosswalk, all four lined up, stomping their boots up and down like ponies.

"You should have kept that list, Collette," said Daddy. "To remember this special day."

Collette smiled, shaking her head. She wouldn't need the list to remember today. She would remember every minute of the twelve hours.

Especially the last part she would spend with her brothers and little sister.

They would be noisier, more confusing, and crazier than the other hours. Maybe Stevie would spill his eggnog, Laura would probably bump into the train table and knock things over, and Jeff would get mad if he didn't get to start the trains for the first time.

But they would still be the best hours — the hours that would make Christmas finally arrive at the Murphy house.

Collette raced ahead, swatting the snowflakes with both arms. She suddenly felt like the Christmas angel set free from the tree.

"It sure feels like Christmas to me now," she laughed, turning to smile at Sarah and her parents.

"Feels like the best Christmas of all."